Ruby in the Water

A NOVEL

J. P. STERLING

ISBN: 978-0-9984421-0-5

J.P. Sterling

Copy Editor: Ellen Violette

Special Bonus Offer – Two Free Gifts

Thank you for your interest in Ruby in the Water.

Download a FREE chapter to "Lily in the Stone", the sequel book to "Ruby in the Water"

And

A complementary PDF "Ruby in the Water Behind the Scenes Fun Facts" at

http://www.jpsterlingauthor.com/free/

Warning: Both gifts contain plots spoilers to "Ruby in the Water".

Dedication

This book is dedicated to my son. You are my inspiration.
I love you for always – no matter what.

Acknowledgements

When I decided to write a book, I asked God to pave the way. I asked him to put the right people in my life, and I am still amazed at how the process has unfolded. One by one, I had new mentors fall into my life at the exact perfect moment that I needed them. I can't name everyone, but I need to name a few: Amanda, Brooks, Jonathan, Betsy, Sara, Ellen, and of course my husband.

One

Tonight was "the night" – imperative to seventeen-year-old Peter Arnold's career. It was opening night of his first headlining tour to promote his classical piano album, *Ruby in the Water*. Backstage in his dressing room, Peter slid his arms into the sleeves of his pressed tuxedo shirt and tucked it into his pants. He reached into the inside front pocket of his jacket to retrieve his monogrammed cufflinks and pinned his French cuffs closed. He glanced in the mirror briefly. A recent haircut left his blond hair too short to reveal the soft wave in his hair. Whisker stubble shadowed his baby face.

A fan hummed on a nearby table. The metal rattled as it shook from being on uneven legs. *I'm gonna chuck that fan out the window.* Peter reached behind it, turning the knob to the "Off" position. He closed his eyes and breathed slowly trying to center himself. A loud rapping on Peter's dressing-room door echoed inside the room. He leaned heavily on his cane with his left hand as he ambled to the door and opened it to see Anne, his mother, standing there out of breath. Peter's six-year-old twin siblings trailed behind her. Peter opened the door wider for his family to enter the room.

"Are you feeling okay?" Anne asked as she plopped down on the sofa against the wall, grabbed the TV remote, and turned on the cartoon channel for the twins. One of the twins, Johnny, curled up next to Anne on the couch. The other twin, Macey, played on the floor with a doll she had brought with her.

"Yeah, I'm a little tired, but I think it's all the commotion." Peter leaned against the arm of the couch his mom was sitting on.

"The commotion? Or, do you mean the emotion? The emotion commotion?" Anne said as she looked at Peter with a huge proud mom grin on her face while she smoothed Johnny's hair with her hand.

"Definitely the emotion commotion." Peter forced a smile for his mother even though he was feeling lightheaded from the migraine headache he had all week.

"Did you eat anything?"

"I ate that sandwich earlier."

"That was this morning, you need to have something else. Here, drink some of my coconut water. It has Acai and probiotics in it. It should give you energy." Anne pulled the bottle from her purse, holding it out to Peter.

Peter turned his head to glare at his mom. "Mom, you know I don't drink anything before a show."

"Yeah, I know, but you don't look well. Here, do you want one of my B-vitamins?" Anne reached into her briefcase-sized, black-leather mom purse to grab her vitamin pouch. Raising seven kids, mostly by herself, had made Anne a nutritionist, among many other things.

"No, I think I need some fresh air," Peter said. "You guys make yourselves at home here. I'm gonna run out back to breathe a little before I've gotta go out there. Those lights always get so stinking hot." Peter's back spasmed when he stood. His shoulder's stiffened from the force. It was a pain he had been feeling on and off for weeks. He tried to ignore it, hoping it would go away. *I just have to get through the next three hours, and then I can lie down.* He hung his cane in the closet and closed the door concealing it.

"Okay." Anne folded her bottom lip under as she observed Peter.

"I'll tell Sammy to come grab you when it's time to get to your seats," Peter said as he turned to walk out the door, but he felt Anne's hand on his shoulder.

"Why are you walking like that? Do you need me to grab your cane again?" she asked as she was now standing behind him.

"My back's just a little tight; I think walking might loosen it up. I'm not using my cane out there." *Too many photographers would love to see that.* Peter's piano talent gave him the confidence he needed to get through life, but underneath the façade he was an insecure teenager with a disability who just wanted to fit in. Using a walking cane fell into one of the areas in his life that brought out his insecurities.

Peter left his mom standing with her eyebrows furrowed. He grimaced through the back spasms as he hung onto the hallway wall on his search for fresh air. Peter knew there was a private loading dock off the back exit. In the hallway, he bumped into his manager, Sammy. "Why are you not in your tails?" Sammy asked. "It's time to go." Sammy was one of those guys who thought a black-leather jacket was appropriate for every occasion. He would grease his dark hair back, which made his brown eyes look beady and his nose look extra pointy.

I don't think I'm the one who needs to worry about looking classy. "I just need some air; I'm really warm."

"We don't have time for air. I'll grab you a bottle of water to drink on the way down to the stage entrance. We can stop and grab your tails on the way." Sammy used his right hand to usher Peter in the opposite direction.

"You know I don't drink water before I play." Peter's rolled his eyes. "Can I have a few moments outside to catch my breath?"

"Do you want to be even a little late for the biggest night of your career? There's dozens of critics in the audience tonight waiting to swallow every mistake you make, just so they can regurgitate it up later in a bad review in the morning."

"Well, when you put it that way, I guess I can wait until after the show." Peter grudgingly turned around to walk back. "Can you help my family to their seats? I got them front-row tickets tonight," Peter asked as they stepped back into his dressing room for his tails. His dad, Thomas, and Peter's three other brothers: twelve-year-old Shiloh, nineteen-year-old Tane, and twenty-year-old Paul had shown up, finally. The only family member missing was Peter's sister, Marie, but she was overseas on her yearly mission trip. Peter's family visited loudly as they enjoyed the rare evening out together.

"Hey guys, I have to go on now. Sammy's going to help you to your seats," Peter shouted over their voices as he stretched his arm into his coat sleeve. He let out a heavy breath with the new layer of dense clothes as he tugged at his collar to loosen it.

"Good luck! We love you!" A chorus of good wishes sang from his family as they filed out the door. Anne was the last one to hug Peter; she lingered in their embrace and left him with a wink.

Peter didn't have time to get nervous before the show. Piano was an exhalation to him – an automatic release like a reflex. The hardest part of performing was right after the lights dimmed. A singular white spotlight illuminated the piano, inviting him over. He liked to wait a few moments for his eyes to adjust to the light before he walked out onto the stage.

While he waited, he rubbed each of his finger joints one last time to ensure they were limber. Cerebral palsy was a cruel enemy to his joints. It was only the repetitive motion of playing piano that loosened his joints enough to open them up all the way, allowing them to gain strength and become *almost* normal. Piano opened Peter up in many ways that even went beyond the physical; it exposed his soul. It was a lifeline through childhood, giving him a positive focus. It drowned out the critics who called him a brat. It gave him an identity.

Tonight, walking out to the piano, he was handsome in his dark suit with his lady-killer blue eyes. Always walking with at least a limp, he slowly strode to steady his weak legs. Struck by the intensity of the applause, which exploded, he felt the stage floor vibrate beneath his feet.

Peter was grateful for his fans. There were a lot of them as he had been playing publicly since he was in kindergarten. His disability layered with his dramatic delivery, made the industry covet him – he was their unicorn. *This is the moment my dreams come true.* He briefly glanced around, waved, and then sat down in his normal position at the piano. Without pause, he struck his first chord. Peter swayed into the music as he reached for the keys. His back spasms worsened. He sucked in air and stiffened, unable to relax. A few loud, disorganized cords bombed out of the piano.

Peter felt a constricting pain in his lower back, unlike any of the previous ones. It sucked all breath from his chest. *Not now,* he cried inwardly. *I've got to push through it.* Unable to get enough oxygen, or forgive the pain, which felt like his interior flesh was twisting into knots, he had no choice but to give in to it. He keeled over onto his side, and then all the way onto the ground. Grabbing his back as he laid on the cold stage in the fetal position, he cried.

Anne leaped from her seat and ran to her son. His father, Thomas, was right behind her. The audience buzzed with hushed whispers.

"Peter! Can you hear me?" Anne had crawled up next to him on the stage floor with her face pushed inches from his.

"My back hurts," he winced. *I think I'm going to die.*

Thomas, a trained physician, leaned in assessing him, "It's your kidneys. We need to get you out of here. Can you walk?"

Peter screamed as to confirm there would be no walking. Without wasting another second, Thomas scooped up Peter like a new baby and carried him out the stage entrance with the family trailing behind him. "Shiloh, take my phone. Call the hospital ER. Tell them I'm on my way down there. Ask for Dr. Greyon and Dr. Arbeck. Paul, can you take everyone home in Anne's van? I'll go with your mom and Peter in my car. I'll call you when we know more." Thomas hollered out instructions to Peter's brother, Paul, as he ran down the corridor and out the back door.

Peter's cries weakened. "He's passing out," Thomas said. "We need to hurry." They ran to the car and as they were getting Peter settled in the backseat, Sammy approached them.

"What do I do?" Sammy asked.

"Tell them the show's over," Thomas said. "But first, you're going to drive us to the ER. He tossed the keys and made his intentions clear. "Floor it." Thomas crawled in the back seat and laid Peter's head in his lap to monitor his vitals. Anne jumped in shotgun and barely shut her door before the tires squawked so loudly two cars in the nearby intersection slammed their breaks in confusion.

Peter saw the roof of the car, barely. His pain was easing now, but everything seemed so hazy. Sounds became muffled and unrecognizable, and then a blur. Somewhere in the distance, Peter heard a church organ groan out a concluding "Ave Maria" as parishioners herded themselves out the back door of his church. He was dreaming now. It was an automatic dream sequences he had his whole life. It haunted him, calling him toward her – like a magnetic field. As always, the dream replayed succinctly and without pause.

In this particular dream, the Arnold family gathered in the first three pews of their church, watching Father Raymond prepare the baptismal fountain for a sacrament of initiation. The fountain was carved from an emerald marble which appeared unaged, but was at least a century old. Peter watched Anne run her fingers over the fount's curved stone as if she couldn't help but admire its aesthetics.

"Peter! Stop kicking the pew!" ten-year-old Marie whispered from the bench straight in front of five-year-old Peter. Peter sat next to his two older brothers: eight-year-old Tane and nine-year-old Paul, who were also annoyed at Peter's fidgeting.

Discontinuing the kicking, Peter instead made noises competing with Father's opening prayer. "ZZZZimmmmmummmm-abababababbadoooolama," he rocked his head back and forth, fanning out his overgrown blond mop of hair. *This is soooo boring to sit here. It's fun to bug Marie,* he thought.

"Can't you be quiet and sit still?" Marie said. Peter spotted his mother out of the corner of his eye and she was giving him "the look". She stood up front because she was going to be Nixon's Godmother, but she was keeping an eye on everything, and she was not happy. She was more than halfway through another difficult pregnancy, and her patience was slim when it came to Peter's behavior in public.

"I have to go to the bathroom," Peter said.

"Shh! No, not now. You'll have to wait until this is over," Marie said.

"I have to go."

"You have to wait." Marie grew even more impatient. Peter's tone changed from whining to crying. With scarlet-colored ears, Anne glared at them from up front, pointing for Marie to take her brother out of the church. Peter knew his mom was annoyed, *but I have to pee.*

Connected to the church was a door leading to a vacant school. The school had been consolidated with another school in the district, but the parish still used their bathrooms. Peter marched on through the empty hallway to the men's room, knowing exactly where the bathroom was located because it was a regular Sunday stop for him.

After using the facilities, Peter stopped at the water fountain to play with the water. Giggling fiercely, he drenched his Sunday shirt and his pants with water. Even the top of his hair spiked from being wet. *This is sweet! It splashes up like a waterfall.*

"Stop it! You're soaked. Mom's going to be so mad at you," Marie scolded.

"I'm hot. I don't want to go back." Peter wiggled into the corner to avoid being caught and scrunched down his body in protest. Suffering from cerebral palsy, he had to wear leg braces to assist him with walking. The braces steadied his ankles as they cradled his feet and stretched to just below his knees. Scrunching down took extra effort, but he was so determined to pout, he found a way. Peter looked to Marie and saw she was smiling. Peter had an effect on people. Even when he should have been trouble, he knew how to melt hearts with his simple innocence.

Peter saw something out the window. "A slide!" He shot up, took two seconds to balance himself, and ran out into the church backyard where a small playground rested. He was halfway up the slide steps when Marie raced out behind him, screaming. Peter ignored her. He was in his happy place, climbing the stairs and singing nonsense tunes.

"You'd better get down or the Goat Woman is gonna come over here to pluck your feet right off your legs!"

"WEEEEEEEEEEE," sang Peter on his way down the slide. "What's a Goat Woman?"

"It's the lady who lives in the house on the hill." Marie pointed at a decrepit-looking house set up on the hill behind the church. Peter had never been allowed on the playground before so he had not noticed the house. He looked at the house and its surroundings. The church was in a slightly rural setting on the edge of town and behind it were rolling prairie hills. Evergreen trees freckled the surface of the hills on one side and grew thick on the other side. The house was slightly camouflaged as it sat on the edge of the first tree row.

"There's no Goat Woman. I don't see anyone." Peter sucked in his lower lip.

"That's because she usually only comes out at night. She sneaks up on people when they're not expecting it," Marie explained. "You have never heard the legend of the Goat Woman?"

Peter stared at his sister, "No, I don't know what you're talking about."

"I'll tell you it then," Marie paused, lowed her voice and squinted her eyes, "The Goat Woman looks normal enough, at first. She always wears a long gray robe with her black stringy curls hanging in a mess all over her head, hiding part of her face. She rarely goes anywhere, but sometimes, you can spot her roaming those hills. Her top half is normal like us, beautiful in fact. People have said her face looks like a porcelain doll without a smile.

However, if you look closely at her, you will see she does not have normal-person feet. Attached to her lower leg, she has the hooves of a goat. She tries to hide them under her robe, but sometimes, you can see her black-animal hooves peek out. That's not the worst part." Marie paused to catch Peter's eyesight and continued, "Her appetite's like a goat; she'll eat anything in her way from tin cans to the clothes you're wearing." Marie leaned over right next to Peter's ear and in a voice barely above a whisper, she continued, "Her favorite thing to eat, though, is little-people feet because *feet* are what she desires the most in life."

Peter swallowed hard and looked at his legs and feet. His wobbly legs and his slightly bent left foot were not much to desire. He swallowed again trying to clear the lump in his throat. *She wouldn't want my feet. . .*

Marie continued, "She used to prey on little kids at the school here and that's why they shut it down. Too many parents didn't like how close she was to their kids. I guess there was an 'incident' a few years back. Now, she waits all alone in her cabin for unknowing kids to come a little too close." Marie's eyes popped open wide and she screamed, "Look out!" Peter felt someone pulling him backwards and down to the ground. Falling all the way back, he looked up and saw her face, her glowing green eyes— it was the Goat Woman!

Two

ANNE

Transporting Peter to the emergency room was the easiest part of the next few hours. Upon arrival, Thomas and Anne were pushed out of the way and restricted to the waiting room. They watched hospital staff push Peter's white rolling cot out of the corridor through two heavy, metal doors. The clanking of the doors closing left the room in silence. Anne stared at Thomas with wide eyes looking for answers in Thomas's own brown eyes but he had no answers. It was time to wait.

The footsteps and voices of people bustling down the hall muffled together in the background as Anne kept her ears attuned, waiting for the clang of the door to reopen with news. "Can you call someone to tell us what's going on in there? A nurse maybe?" Anne asked Thomas.

"No, nurses can't legally update family on a patient's status, and it'll take more than a few moments to properly diagnose. They'll tell us as soon as they know," Thomas muttered.

"Well, not officially update us of course, but since you work here you must know someone who can just tell us what's going on in there," Anne pressed.

"Anne, please don't make this worse than it has to be. This is protocol. Family waits in the *waiting room* until the doctors can talk to them. I'm a doctor, yes, but not a magician. I hate this just as much as you." Thomas grabbed Anne's hand.

"Sorry, I'm just worried," Anne sighed as she retreated into her head. *We're supposed to be on a bus right now to start Peter's tour. This was supposed to be one of the happiest days of our lives.*

Closing her eyes, Anne shuddered at her recent memory of Peter's face hanging to the side as the nurses rolled him away. *Please baby open your eyes for me,* she had prayed, but he never did. She thought it was ironic how many times she had prayed in desperation during Peter's younger years for him to just *close* his eyes and keep them closed so he would sleep, and now the thought of them closed terrified her.

From her memory, she could almost hear his sweet voice calling out to her from across the hall after he had woken up, yet again, from another nightmare. In her daydream, Anne remembered it all too well.

*   *   *

"Mom! Mommy!" An urgent voice had cried from across the hall. Rolling over, Anne slid her feet out of bed and onto the floor, robotically walking towards the voice as she had done thousands of times. Once in the hall, she glanced at the microwave in the kitchen and it read 12:45 a.m. *A whooping forty-five minutes since I got Peter to go to sleep,* she thought as she made a mental note to just stay with Peter because she would not do the back and forth stuff tonight.

Anne peeked into his room. A five-year-old Peter sat up in his bed with big tears running down his face. She crawled up next to him, laid her head on his pillow, and patted the spot next to her head for him to lie down too. He cuddled her, and still sobbing, his tears quickly tickled Anne's cheek. She reached out to rub his back and whispered, "You're okay."

"It's the gowonan," he said as he sobbed.

"Um?"

"The Goat Woman," he annunciated better.

"The Goat Woman again?"

"Yeah, she's really scary."

"Peter, we've talked about this before. There's nothing scary about the Goat Woman. She's called that because she literally used to raise goats, and they lived on the hill with her. Everyone saw them, so they called her the Goat Woman."

"You know her?"

Anne paused for a long time unable to find a better way to explain the Goat Woman. "I knew her a while ago. She's harmless, Peter. Do you think Father Raymond would be okay with letting someone live there if they were bad?"

"No, I guess not."

"So, do you think we can we go to sleep now?"

"Okay, but I've gotta go to the bathroom."

"Alright, go ahead, but hurry up."

After a few short minutes, a drifting Anne heard Peter tiptoe back into the room. Anne felt Peter snuggle in next to her and pulled her arm on his tummy – something he had done since he was a little nursling. Giving herself permission to relax, she let herself fall into a light sleep. A moment later, she was pulled from her sleep by little fingers digging into her arm, quiet sobs, and something else: a warm, wet sensation on her stomach.

You peed the bed again. I still have a pile of sheets from last night I need to wash. She opened her heavy eyelids. Mechanically from habit, she sat up and reached for Peter's blanket piled on the other side of the bed. She straightened it out and checked it to make sure it wasn't wet. Anne held the blanket up against her chest for Peter to snuggle into as she pulled him out of bed. She walked to the dresser, grabbed dry pajamas and underpants, and changed him. She glanced at the clock, which now read, 2:10 a.m. Peter still sobbed softly, and up until this point, Anne thought it was because he was wet, but under his quiet sobs she heard about the Goat Woman.

"Honey, there's no lady who's gonna hurt you." Anne noticed even though Peter was sobbing, he was still half asleep. *I just need to be quiet and get him back to bed before he wakes all the way up.* Glancing at the soiled sheets, she decided to ignore them – as she just didn't have the energy for it now – she sighed and carried Peter back into her bedroom. They both snuggled into the bed next to Peter's dad. As Peter fell back to sleep, Anne heard a quiet, "I sorry mama" and then silence, and then she was asleep.

"Mom, mom." Once again, Anne felt little fingers digging into her arm. Without opening her eyes, exhausted tears started to well up inside her closed eyelids, but she tried to tamp them down so Peter wouldn't be stimulated. "Mom, dad's snoring and I can't sleep."

Anne caught a glimpse of the red alarm clock, 3:04 a.m. *If I get him back to sleep now, I can still get at least another hour or two of sleep.* She picked Peter up with his blanket and carried him out to the couch in the living room. She shoved over a pile of newspapers. She picked up the laundry basket, which had sat centered on the couch and placed it on the coffee table. Lying down, she pulled Peter up next to her side and tried to snuggle.

"Mom."

"Shh, sleepy time Peter."

"Mom."

This was a typical night with Peter's overactive imagination. Hearing every noise, he would wake up if you dropped a sock. Anne hadn't gotten a full night of sleep since Peter arrived into their family. "Peter, mommy's tired. If you can't sleep just lie here with your eyes closed until the sun comes in the window over there."

Peter stayed still until the first speck of light crept inside the living room and then he whispered, "Mom. It's morning. Mom, it's light." Anne opened one eye. Through the curtain, she could see a faint lightening of the darkness, but it was still mostly dark. She glanced at the clock on the wall; it was 4:57 a.m.

Peter wiggled his way out of Anne's snuggle until he could roll onto the floor; he crawled over to the toy chest in the corner and pulled out his Lego's. Anne exhaustedly called from the couch, "You play quietly and stay right here while I rest –" She fell back asleep.

Crash!

Anne jolted awake and looked to find Peter huddled in a ball on the floor under the window. His arms wrapped around his chest, hugging himself while he sobbed. Anne got off the couch and walked over to Peter, "What's going on?"

"The Goat Woman! She's outside. I looked out the window to see if the sun was out and she was standing on the sidewalk, staring at the house."

Anne sighed. Scared to look at the clock, she knew she was up for the day now. She pulled the curtain aside, looking out. Down the block there was a silhouette of someone walking. It was too foggy to make out any distinct features, but the figure looked to be carrying a red-plastic bag. He or she didn't look scary – just a person walking past. She turned away, and then saw the clock: 6:11 a.m. *That's what I was afraid of. This's going to be a long day.* She knelt next to Peter and smoothed his hair. "How are your hands this morning? Do you need me to rub them?"

"Yeah, just this one's locked." Peter held up his right hand revealing a middle finger, ring finger, and pinky finger curled into a fist. Anne took his hand into hers and twisted her fingers around his joints, massaging them until she felt the tension release. Peter stared at the wall while she kneaded them.

"There you go. How about a bowl of oatmeal?" Anne asked as she laid his hand on his lap. Peter grinned and went to sit at the table, waiting for his mom to get out a bowl. Naturally caffeinated, he was talking away.

"Mom, I heard the Goat Woman outside. I saw her, and I heard her walk by." His eyes were large as quarters.

"It was just a person walking by," Anne said. Peter's brothers, Paul and Tane, had entered the kitchen for breakfast. They got in on the conversation just to tease Peter.

"I bet it was her," Tane said as he shoved a spoon filled with colored marshmallow cereal into his mouth. He was still in his pajamas and his dark hair was spiked in the back from where he had slept. "What did she look like?"

Peter stopped eating his oatmeal as he now stared at Tane. "She was wearing her robe, and she had a trash bag."

"What color was the bag?" Tane asked.

"Red," Peter said.

"Yep, that's her. She's half goat. She eats trash. She digs in people's garbage's while they sleep, so she can get food."

"How can she eat garbage?" Peter asked.

"That's how goats are. You better hope she doesn't like your garbage because if she does, she might come back to get your feet," Tane said. Paul laughed so hard he snorted, and milk from his cereal dripped out of his mouth, running down on his chin.

"Why would she want my feet?" Peter asked.

"Cause your feet are all twisted up like her crazy brain –"

"Enough!" Anne interrupted as she clinched her hands into fists. *I know where this is going.* She glared at Tane, and then smoothed out the top of Peter's hair. "Peter, your brother's making this up. He just wants to scare you," Anne said. "Let's find something else to chat about. Who wants eggs?"

Peter's eyes shifted from his mother to his brother. Quietly he said, "I'll have eggs, please."

Peter was finishing his second breakfast of eggs and ketchup by the time Thomas came into the kitchen and he was dressed for work. Thomas was a family-practice doctor who worked long shifts. Anne hated how long his shifts were because she had no backup with the kids. She knew not to complain though because Thomas was a workaholic who felt his obligation was just to provide for his family.

"Well, look who's up to get the worm this morning," Thomas said.

Peter frowned and looked at his eggs, "You think there's worms in my eggs?"

"No," Peter's dad chuckled, "That's just a saying, which means you're up early. No worms in your eggs." He turned and looked at Anne. "I need to leave now because I have a meeting. I'll see you tonight."

Anne kissed Thomas goodbye, and then hurried to get the kids into her van. All three of her boys went to the same elementary school. Peter attended school in the afternoon four days a week since he was only in Kindergarten. After Anne dropped Paul and Tane off at their school, she drove all the way across town to drop Marie off at the middle school. Many mornings after the kids were dropped off at their locations, Anne and Peter made a third stop to their favorite coffee and tea shop; today would be one of those days.

As they drove, Peter sat in the back seat in his car seat, making engine noises. "Mom, I gotta go the bathroom."

"I thought I told you to go before we left? Can you wait until we get to Steep & Brew?"

"I'll try, but hurry."

"I'm on it!" Anne pretended to drive faster by mimicking Peter's engine noises. Peter cracked up in the back seat, and they were both laughing silly by the time they pushed through the heavy, wood door at Steep & Brew. Anne nodded her head toward Peter to go find the bathroom. He trotted up the handicapped ramp, mimicking a racecar motor revving the whole way.

Anne ordered her favorite frosted maple latte and a chocolate steamer with only half the sugar syrup for Peter. She looked around while she waited for Peter to return. Steep & Brew was the cutest coffee shop because it was set up in a 19th-century church. The ceiling was vaulted and the old alter was built up into the counter that the staff worked behind. All the original wood work had been redone into a gorgeous dark, cherry finish and the windows were arched with stained glass. The tables were matched with the original pews for seating. They always had fresh art hanging on the walls from local artists, and the best classics set out to be read; there was a fish tank near the door.

"Fishy," Anne heard Peter say and she turned and saw her son making a fish face as he pointed to the tank. Their regular routine was to look at the fish while they waited for their drinks. Making fish faces at each other, they studied the tank and noticed the different things in its' interior. A few months ago, someone put a metal ornament into the tank, which had a matching magnet. The magnet could be placed against the glass to catch the metal ornament, and you could drag the ornament along the inside of the glass. Peter loved playing with it as he watched how the fish interacted with the moving ornament.

In a previous visit, Peter was playing with the magnet and ornament, and the ornament fell too far into the interior of the tank. The magnet wasn't strong enough to catch it, so the ornament just sat there immobile. Every single time they came to Steep & Brew since the ornament fell too far inside, they had to check to see if it had moved. Peter was so persistent that he would still ask for the magnet, and point to the ornament, and didn't understand why it didn't move.

"It's broken," Anne said for what felt like the hundredth time, explaining the situation.

"No."

"Yes, it doesn't work," she repeated, as she looked for something else to distract him before he had a meltdown. "Look at the fishy."

"No, I want that." Peter pointed at the magnet, "I want that magnet."

"It's broken. Look at the fishy." She pointed at the fish and she saw someone had dumped a plastic-looking ruby into the tank. It rested by itself as a singular ruby shimmering on top of the white gravel rocks. *There's a ruby in the water.* Just as she thought the phrase, she heard how poetic it sounded; *Ruby in the water. It sounds like a song title.* "Ruby in the water." She pointed it out for Peter.

"Ruby."

"Yep, ruby in the water," Repeating the phrase again because she loved the way it sounded, Anne imagined a song about a person who was special and stuck out from everyone else – like the ruby stood out from the gravel rock. She imagined a song, which could very well describe Peter, her little ruby in the water.

"Up! Up!" Peter said. Anne jolted backwards from someone bumping into her. She looked down to see a stressed Peter grabbing at her neck and sticking his foot on her hip, trying to climb her. A man had walked in the door and was standing next to them, looking down at a newspaper. Peter, ever slow to warm up to anyone, demanded to be held by someone he trusted, usually Anne. Once in Anne's arms, he hid his face in her chest and peeked out at the man. Peter had always clung to Anne when he was scared. He didn't get scared as much as he used to, but he was good at reading people, and every occasionally, he would get a vibe. "Make me invisible mom," he whispered.

"Okay," she whispered back. She reached into her purse, pulled out a pair of sunglasses and placed them on Peter's face. She began to sing in a whisper, directly into his ear, a song she made up a while ago once when he was hiding on her like he was now.

Make me invisible, I don't want to see,

This man behind me, staring at me

Lord, can you help me, help me be brave.

I need you, I need to be saved.

Anne made up this song to help Peter understand his emotions. *I'm going to finish writing it one day when I have some time to sit down and think,* she always thought to herself whenever she sang it. She knew the first verse would be about a little boy who hides on his mom from strangers, just like Peter did. The second verse would be about an older boy doing something embarrassing, or getting into trouble, or something that would make him want to run. The third verse would be about a young man on his first date with his future wife and how he was nervous. The last verse would be about an old man dying and he calls out that he doesn't want see death coming for him. She had it all planned. *Someday when the kids are grown, I'll write this song.* She was not a songwriter, a singer, or even a poetic, but she had dreams that went beyond being a housewife.

"Can you see me?" Peter whispered.

"Nope. Just hold onto my neck so I don't lose you," Anne pretended. Anne added the glasses to the song about a year ago, and told Peter if she sang the song while he wore the glasses he would be invisible. It really helped calm his nerves, so they used this routine often. When Peter was ready to be seen, he would just have to remove his glasses.

"Oh, that's us, Peter. They're calling our drinks; let's go. We should grab them and get going. We have an errand to run before I take you back to school."

Three

The clanking of the door whipped Anne from her daydream, bringing her eyes to focus on the two doctors walking towards her and Thomas. She jumped to her feet. Thomas recognized the men as: Dr. Greyon and Dr. Arbeck, the two physicians he had requested. Dr. Arbeck was from India and had a thick accent, so he allowed Dr. Greyon to do most of the talking.

"How is he?" Anne blurted out.

Dr. Greyon motioned for Anne to sit. Anne sat and Thomas greeted the doctors by shaking their hands. Dr. Greyon asked, "Do you want the good news or the bad news first?"

"Why do they always ask this at hospitals?" Anne questioned.

"They don't always ask. Sometimes there's no good news, so you don't get a choice," Thomas replied. "We want the good news first."

Dr. Greyon sat across from them with his feet planted firmly on the ground. "The good news is we have him stabilized, but sedated. He won't wake up, and we're going to keep him like that until we can get his pain under control."

"That's good news?" Anne asked.

"Yes, it's good news because he's alive and he's feeling little, if any, pain right now," Dr. Greyon said as he stared back at Anne.

"Okay, what's the bad news?" Anne asked, terrified of the answer. Thomas reached for her hand, squeezing it hard.

"Well, your son's ill, and by the look of all the tests we ran, he's been sick for a while. Has he said anything to either of you?" Dr. Greyon's eyes bounced from Thomas to Anne.

"No, I thought he looked tired, but I thought it had to do with the stress of everything," Anne explained and looked to Thomas to comment.

"I didn't notice anything out of the ordinary although Peter has always had a weaker immune system. Headaches and lethargy are something he continuously battles alongside his cerebral palsy. And, of course, you know about his urinary issues. He's never been able to get those functioning normally," Thomas said.

Dr. Greyon spoke, "Peter's body's flooded with infection. I found four organ infections in just the tests we ran, but I would think there are more."

Anne interrupted, "Four? Where?" She nervously played with her purse strap as she waited for the answer.

"There's infection in his lungs, his heart, his liver, and his gall-bladder. Like I said, there may be more. Basically, his whole body's under attack by bacteria right now. His temperature was right under 105 degrees when you brought him in," Dr. Greyon said. He paused to make sure they were listening, and then continued, "I wish I could say that is the worst of it. . ."

"It's his kidneys, right?" Anne interrupted.

Nodding, Dr. Greyson continued, "Yes, I'm afraid we have to mention kidney failure. His liver appears to have been working overtime to compensate for his weak kidneys, and he has taxed his liver as well."

"What does this all mean?" Anne asked.

"There's a lot going on. When one part of the body's not working, something must compensate. Then, that part of the body starts to malfunction and something else must compensate. It's like a house of cards. . ."

"Please, just tell me what this means," Anne pleaded.

"We're treating the infection intravenously with antibiotics. His immune system's too weak to fight it alone, but with the medicine, we should clear up all the infection. We're going to start dialysis on him, but," he paused to make sure he held Anne's eye contact. "He needs a transplant."

Breathing heavy as if a truck had landed in her lungs, Anne repeated, "A transplant." She looked to Thomas, who nodded in agreement with what the doctors were saying.

"We knew it would probably come to this. When does he need it?" Thomas rubbed his hand on his chin.

"Yesterday," Dr. Greyon spoke frankly.

"How do we get a kidney?" Anne looked at Thomas.

"We have to find a donor."

"I'll do it. Please take mine." Anne looked back to Dr. Greyon.

"The first thing we need to do is get the blood-type matched. Peter's Type O Negative. Do you know which of you is O?"

"I'm A Positive," Thomas said.

"Then you should be the O. He has to get it from one of you," Dr. Greyon looked at Anne.

The color in her face drained. "I have to be Type O to give a kidney?"

"Yes, to be a kidney match, you need to make sure the blood type of the donor matches. That's the first step. With Peter, he has some special considerations, and we would like to limit his kidney donor to immediate family only – most likely a parent. It would limit his risk of rejection. His body's too weak to risk a nonrelative."

"Okay, I'll do it," Anne said as her throat tightened. *Oh, please Lord, don't let this come down to this. I can't lose him now.*

Dr. Greyon nodded. "Good. We'll be moving Peter into his own room in intensive care as soon as dialysis is finished. It should be another couple of hours before we have him settled, and then if you would like to see him, that should be okay."

"Yes, please. I want to see him as soon as possible," Anne said.

"We'll make sure we notify you. In the meantime, we can send you to the lab and get started on your blood work. We really don't want to waste any time getting a donor lined up. It's all very premature to go into details, but if we're able to go forward with the procedure, we'll sit down with the full-disclosure details," Dr. Greyon said. Both doctors stood up.

"Thank you," Thomas said and stood, offering a second handshake to the doctors before they left.

"Thomas, I feel like I'm going to be ill," Anne said. "Is it really coming to this?"

"I'm afraid so. Let's just do one day at a time." Thomas embraced Anne. He ran his fingers through the back of her golden hair, smelling her vanilla shampoo.

"I need to call the kids and give them an update again. I'll tell them to wait until tomorrow to come visit though."

"Anne, it's tomorrow. It's after 6:00 a.m. The lab just reopened for the day."

Anne's eyes popped wide open as she pulled away from Thomas and turned to look at the clock behind her. Being in the hospital had warped her sense of time.

Moments later, Anne was at the lab waiting to get her blood drawn. Her stomach felt like ocean waves were bouncing at the bottom of it, flipping it inside out. "I really don't feel well, Thomas," Anne said as she fanned herself for air.

"Did you eat anything today?" Thomas asked.

"No, I haven't eaten today. I didn't eat much yesterday either. I was saving my calories for the celebration after the concert. I even baked a cake." Saddened by the memory of what would have been a celebration, Anne looked down as she finished talking.

"Why don't you go grab a juice, and maybe a piece of toast before they draw your blood, or you'll get sick," Thomas said but then stood up. "Oh, never mind, I'll do it. I can run through the employee line; it's a lot faster. Wait here," he said as he left.

I'm going to hurl all over this floor. It's too bad. It looks like it was just waxed. If I throw up, it'll be worse than the last time I threw up in public. Trying to forget about the bigger issue, she allowed herself to daydream. *The last time I got sick in public was over a decade ago when I was pregnant with Shiloh.*

● ● ●

It had been in the afternoon right after Anne dropped Peter off for his half day of kindergarten, and she decided to get some groceries. Anne rounded a corner with a stuffed, grocery cart. She stopped to grab a roll of paper towels and knocked a stack over with her baby belly, eight months huge. Nauseated from the pregnancy, it was excruciating being in a grocery store. As she collected the towels and restacked them, her cell phone rang. The caller ID confirmed it was Peter's school.

Kindergarten had been a rough transition for everyone in Peter's path. Peter was the second youngest in his class as he had a July birthday, and he wasn't adjusting well. It had been a few months, but they were all still in the process of working out the knots, which occurred regularly. Anne now referred to the school as "Peter's school" because whenever someone called, it was about Peter.

"Hello," Anne answered.

"Mrs. Arnold?"

"Hi Valarie, its Anne." The school secretary, Valerie, and Anne were on a first name basis after the fall they had experienced.

"Yes, hi Anne. I'm calling on behalf of Mrs. Krieg. She needs you to come in here to pick up Peter, and she wants to meet with you while you're here."

"Is Peter alright?"

"Yes, he's fine. I can't say for sure what's going on, but Peter has been in her office again since lunch." Mrs. Krieg was the principal, and she had the most patience with Peter.

"Well, I just visited with her in a meeting last Wednesday. Can I talk to her?" Anne's head was spinning.

"I'm not supposed to say over the phone. You just need to come down here."

"Okay, I'll be right there then." Anne gulped as she hung up the phone. She looked at her cart. She had too many items to put back, and she estimated that it would take another twenty minutes to get everything checked out as she saw only two checkout lines with cashiers, and each line was filled with people. *Valarie didn't say it was an emergency, and I do think she would have said if it were an emergency. . . I'm just going to get checked out now because I don't know when else I can get groceries since going to the store with Peter's a train wreck,* Anne reasoned.

Anne was waiting patiently in line at the checkout when someone lined up behind her with a cart. *Oh no, I smell fried chicken.* The lady behind her had a package of it from the deli. She took a shallow breath in trying not to inhale any chicken. She knew if she gagged, she would have to throw up.

Looking ahead, she noticed there were still two people with packed carts in front of her, and the other checkout lane was closing, so she had nowhere else to go. *Don't think about it,* she told herself. The back of her neck dampened. Anne lifted her hair up and held it with one hand in a makeshift ponytail as she fanned herself with her other hand desperately trying to move the air. Cold sweat trickled down her lower back.

I need a distraction. She looked to the magazine rack. Trembling, her hand could barely flip through an issue of Good Housekeeping. It didn't work. "I gotta go!" she blurted out to the lady who was standing behind her. Frantically fanning herself with one arm and trying to get the cart out of the isle with the other, Anne bolted to the bathroom. Her stomach roared! She felt her cheeks and ears burn red. *I hope no one sees me!*

Her panic doubled when she saw a sign on the women's bathroom door that said, "Out of order". Still fanning her face, Anne turned to go to the men's room and saw a cleaning cart stuck out of the doorway and a sign posted, "Please come back – being cleaned." Anne's deep breathing quickened and she felt like she was hyperventilating. She needed air or a toilet! Panicked, she looked around, but there was nowhere else to go. *The cleaning person isn't even here!* Yanking the cleaning cart out of the doorway with one arm, and now, covering her mouth with her other, she charged in.

"Mam, that bathroom is closed, but . . .," called the lady at the closed checkout lane as she started to follow Anne into the bathroom. Anne didn't care; she was running. The stalls were on the back wall, but the urinals were lined up on the wall closest to her. Choosing the closer of the two facilities, she barely made it to the urinal on the wall before she lost it and puked all over the white marble.

Brown mush oozed down the wall and onto the tile. She wasn't able to bend over a toilet so the vomit ran all the down the front of her dress and even soaked her shoes. Chunks dripped from the tips of her blond curls, which now stuck to the sides of her face. She felt defeated.

"Ma' am," a voice called from the open doorway, and then trailed off as the cashier, whose voice it was, got sight of Anne covered in vomit.

Anne looked back at the woman, knowing she was a hot mess. She felt there was nothing left to do, but laugh. Once she started, she couldn't stop, and she was laughing hysterically. "I'm sorry. I, I, uh, am supposed to be on my way to my son's school for a meeting. I got sick. I'll clean it up," Anne offered after she wiped her face with paper towels she had pulled from the paper towel dispenser.

The cashier smiled, "I saw you were going to be sick. I was trying to get you this." She held up a bag she had grabbed from her checkout, "I didn't think you were going to make it in here." She giggled.

"Nope, you were right," Anne said. Then they both laughed until they had tears in their eyes; it was a lovely bonding moment.

After the laughter died, the cashier spoke, "I'm supposed to be on my break now, but why don't you come back to my till. I'll ring you up so you can get going. I'll have the stock boy come back and clean up this mess."

"Oh, no. I can do it," Anne said.

The lady held up a hand, "Honey, you need a break. Let me help you."

"Thank you." Anne smiled. She did need a break. She could barely handle this interaction covered in humiliation.

Moments later, Anne loaded her van with groceries and glanced at the clock. For Anne, motherhood was always a battle against time. Forty-five minutes had vanished since the school summoned her, and it would take her fifteen minutes to get there if she didn't hit any traffic. She didn't have time to run home to change, but she couldn't go meet with the principal covered in vomit. The stench alone was making her dry heave.

Resourceful, Anne rummaged through the van for something else to slip on. *Four kids and two adults in a household means there has to be something abandoned in here.* She discovered a gym bag full of sweaty, men's clothes, but she quickly discarded it. That, too, nearly made her sick again with the odor of smelly feet. *Oh wait!* There was a white, dress shirt of her husbands'. Thomas always kept a pressed shirt in all the vehicles in case he got called into work when he was out running errands. Today, his need for convenience would save her. Slipping it on over her dress, she was unable to button it over her baby belly, and it was so long that it met the hem of her dress at her knees. She was able to gather the material enough to tie it up above her belly with the excess length.

I don't look too bad for a minivan makeover. Moving on, she looked at her feet. Her white flats had gotten the worst of the vomit, littered with chunks and a fumigating odor that would make a pig cry. Her oldest son, Paul, had a pair of tennis shoes in the van, and she could slip her feet into those, but they were too tight. Anne kept looking. *My boots!* Anne always kept a pair of snow boots in her van, because you just never know what a Minnesota winter will do.

She ran to the back of the van and almost shouted in joy when she found them. They were gray with fur trim and little puff balls. It was nice out today; 65 degrees and no snow. *Maybe I can be in and out before anyone sees my feet? Okay, I'm set,* she thought and drove to the school.

She made it into the front office in one piece, and she could see Mrs. Krieg had her door open. Immediately she identified Peter's loud, boyish laughter. She walked closer to the open door to see Peter and Mrs. Krieg sitting on the floor, playing dinosaurs together.

"No wonder I can't keep him out of your office," Anne called into the doorway.

"Mom!" Peter's whole face lit up when he saw her. He ran over and grabbed her leg for a comfort leg hug.

"Is it snowing?" he asked as he saw her boots.

"No, honey. It's nice out." Peter frowned and gazed at her boots. Anne's stomach was tight. *I don't know why Peter isn't in class, and I feel like a freaking clown standing here in my snow boots with my big pregnant belly.* "Do you need me?" Anne self-consciously looked to Mrs. Krieg.

"Yes." Mrs. Krieg motioned for Anne to come take a seat. "How are you feeling?"

"Umm, okay. Well, sort of. I mean, I feel pregnant, but I'm not sure why I'm here. Can you tell me what's wrong today?" Anne rambled. Anne was normally a confident person except when it came to Peter – he had her whole heart wrapped in his innocence.

"Peter, can you run this box downstairs to the janitor's room in the basement?" Mrs. Krieg asked. The mail had arrived an hour ago; normally, Valerie would sort the mail and leave it in the mailboxes, but Mrs. Krieg snatched the package from Valerie as decoy to get some alone time with Anne. Mrs. Krieg had been an educator for over four decades, and she was always thinking ahead. "You can get a prize out of Valerie's treasure chest when you get back – for being helpful," She added.

"Okay." Peter took the box and left. His dinosaur noises were still on his lips and the two ladies could hear them dissipate as Peter got further away from them. Once they were quiet, Anne's heart sunk. She turned her attention to Mrs. Krieg, smiled, and waited.

"You may remember, we have all-school parent-teacher conferences in two weeks. I wanted to talk to you now about something, so you'll have time to think about it before we all sit down together."

Anne nodded. Mrs. Krieg continued in a low, even tone, "We had another 'incident' this morning, and these incidents are becoming such a regular thing. I think it's time to start thinking about getting Peter some support in the way of medication to help his moods and excessive energy."

"Medicine?" Anne immediately got defensive. "What happened?"

"There was a serious incident in the lunchroom. Peter threw his plate and the plates of the two kids sitting next to him at the wall. He was upset and difficult to calm down. So, the lunchroom attendant sent him up here. I showed him my dinosaurs, and we've been playing, but I didn't mention anything about the lunchroom yet to him. I was hoping we could talk about it together with you here."

"There must have been a reason," Anne said as she knew it didn't sound like something Peter would do unless he was triggered by something.

"Anne," Mrs. Krieg interrupted her thoughts. "Peter will be back shortly, and I'm going to bring this up with him, but I also need to remind you to talk to Mr. Arnold about the treatment. I'll be bringing it up at conference time, and I hope to have a time table for a treatment plan agreed to by then."

"But why? He's a kid. Kids get upset."

Leaning in towards Anne without losing direct eye contact, Mrs. Krieg harshly whispered, "Anne, his teachers are requesting he get a behavior evaluation. They can't keep having these interruptions. We don't have the resources to spend so much time on one kid. Plus, it's not fair to him. The kids see him getting emotional, and he gets singled out as the weak kid. The district's really coming down hard on schools this year to have preventative bullying measures in place. These incidents place a giant target on his back."

Anne chewed on her lip. *I didn't know the teachers complained about him.* Her heart was breaking, but it was interrupted by the sound of Peter outside the door, digging through Valerie's prize box.

"I know you want the best, and trust me Anne, it's time to look at going a step in this direction and getting him some medical support," Mrs. Krieg offered her last advice in a voice hardly above a whisper to shield Peter. Peter returned to the room and stood next to his mom. Mrs. Krieg nodded at Anne to start the conversation, which was a routine they all knew too well.

"Honey, do you know why I'm here?" she asked as she reached out a hand to softly rub his back.

"To take me home again," he answered.

"Yes. Do you know why you have to leave school again before it's over?"

"Cause I hate tuna." He wrinkled his forehead in disgust as he said it.

"Please don't use the word 'hate'. You know, you don't hate anything, but yes, we know you don't *like* tuna, which is why I packed you a bag lunch today. What happened? Did you lose it?"

"They took my bag lunch and made me put tuna on my plate," Peter defended.

Mrs. Krieg interjected, "We have a new policy we started this last quarter, which clearly states you can't bring bag lunches from home. A hot lunch is healthier, and so, in compliance with the policy, the lunch ladies had to discard the bag lunch. They offered him a hot lunch as a substitute."

"What?" Anne snorted out. "Are you kidding me? I never heard about this policy. Peter has a serious food aversion to tuna, which is why I deliberately packed a lunch for him today. You took it from him and forced him to take something he doesn't like?"

"You're making it sound worse than it really was. We have to ensure kids are getting a balanced meal and the only way to monitor it is to require they eat our provided hot lunch."

Anne didn't want to hear about how the school, once again, had to take individual choices away from students and parents. She wanted to grab Peter's hand and run, slamming the door back into Mrs. Krieg's face, but she fought herself. If she had learned anything since Peter enrolled in this school, it was that there was no point in fighting "the system". "So, you got mad that they took your lunch, and threw the one they gave you at the wall?" Anne questioned Peter.

"No, mommy. I tried to be good. I sat at the table with it on my plate, but it smelled so bad. I asked to leave, and the lady said I had to eat three things on my plate before I could. I couldn't even open my mouth to eat anything because the smell of tuna would get in there, and I wanted to throw up. Mommy, I just wanted to leave and they won't let me. I was getting sick, and I needed the tuna smell gone. I didn't mean to make a mess, but I needed the smell *gone* because they wouldn't let me leave," Peter voice cracked as he relived the event.

Anne swallowed hard as she was amazed at the coincidence in occurrences. She couldn't judge him when she basically did the same thing at the grocery store. God's timing was perfect as it made her experience the same thing, allowing her to see the world through his sensitive eyes. She understood how the smell of something could make you want to cry, scream, and get sick. "Honey, we'll talk about this tonight with your father," Anne mustered up a tough mom voice to please Mrs. Krieg, but inside she was dying. She knew the school saw this as a discipline issue, but Anne saw her sensitive little boy who no one understood. "Let's go home," Anne said as she stood, looking at Peter.

Mrs. Krieg handed Anne a bundle of Peter's work to be completed at home. This was getting to be a routine too often as well. Early on, they noticed when Peter would get overwhelmed in the classroom, it was best to remove him for the rest of the day. But now, Anne's mind was starting to click a little differently. *This school didn't have room for individuals. Something needs to change.* Anne pulled her arm around Peter's shoulder and they walked out together in silence. Anne drove the van and took a sharp left to indicate she wasn't going home.

"Where you going?" Peter asked.

"We need a treat from Steep and Brew." Anne smiled into the rear-view mirror, hoping to get Peter to perk up.

"Sweet! I'm starving. Can I get a sandwich too?"

"You sure can. I bet you're hungry since you decided to make wall art with your lunch," she teased. "We'll get it to go, because I still have groceries in the car."

"That's what smells!" Peter said.

Anne tried to smell groceries, but they were all bundled up in the back. She was puzzled for a minute, and then saw her abandoned puke shoes. "No, honey, you smell my morning." Anne slowly chuckled but couldn't contain herself as her laughter broke into a full giggle. "You're not the only one who couldn't handle a food aversion today." Anne dramatically retraced her morning for Peter's entertainment, and they both laughed until they had stomach aches. Gratitude was all she felt for her morning, now, as all the shame and embarrassment was gone. Her eyes were opened to align with the sensitive eyes of her dear Peter.

"So, are you in trouble too?" Peter asked. Anne thought about how nobody yelled at her, and how a nice lady helped her. *Why was it different for kids?* Again, the only thing Anne could come up with was "the system." The school was not handling the situation well; they were wrong.

"Honey, neither one of us is in trouble. It wasn't right for you to throw the tuna, but I understand why you did it. It was a reflex to get it away, so you wouldn't get sick. I know you know not to do that so you're not in trouble. I think we may call those kids tonight and apologize, but having to endure the smell of tuna and embarrassment is probably all the pain you need." Anne couldn't discipline Peter on this one. It just didn't seem like he did anything wrong.

"Thanks, mom."

"You're welcome. For what?"

"For not listening to Mrs. Krieg. You listen to me. You're the only one who gets me. I wish you worked in the lunch room."

Anne's heart broke a little more. In one instance hearing words, as sweet as those would melt her heart, but it was also very sad. After today, she knew them to be the absolute truth; no one else understood him.

Four

"Hey Anne, where are you?" Thomas waved his hand in front of Anne's face.

Blinking her eyes, Anne came out of her daydream about the past and focused on Thomas standing in front of her. "Oh, I didn't see you."

"No kidding, you didn't see me. I was standing here offering you this tray of food and you didn't even look." Thomas set the tray on the table next to Anne. "Are you worried about the test?"

"No, I'm not even thinking about the test. I was thinking about the time I threw up all over the bathroom at the grocery store. It was the day I was supposed to meet Peter's principal."

Thomas nodded. "Yeah, that day was sort of the start of it, wasn't it?"

"Start of what?"

"When we started listening to Peter about how to parent him." Thomas sat down next to Anne and continued, "Look where he has led us."

Anne smiled and grabbed her juice bottle. She noticed the tray Thomas brought her was mauve. It was the same color as the last time she ate hospital food when Peter was in the hospital. *In all the times I have eaten at this hospital – and it has been a lot – I don't ever remember there being a different color food tray. Mauve's so blah.* The lab technician appeared from behind the lab door and escorted Anne back inside the lab for her tests.

"Good Luck." Thomas winked at her. "I'm going outside to call my mom. I'll see you when you're done." Anne nodded and walked through the door. The smell of hand sanitizer hit her first. She sat in a cold chair with her arm resting on the chair arm, ready for the lady to take her blood. Anne's stomach still hadn't settled. After the nurse filled three vials of blood, she was done. Anne reached down to grab her purse, and then rose to her feet; she involuntarily stepped backwards. She grabbed the wall to steady herself.

The lab technician instructed Anne to sit back down. "You can wait here for a few minutes. Do you need me to grab you a juice?"

"No, I actually have one in my purse. I just didn't have time to drink it yet." Anne pulled the juice from her purse, opened it, and took a swig. "I should be okay, and I'm in sort of a hurry."

"Alright, go ahead, but if you start to feel dizzy, please sit down," she said kindly.

Anne nodded. "Thank you." She recognized the "Cover-your-Cough" poster on the door. The pictures of people sneezing and coughing made her want to lather hand sanitizer all over her hands and arms. Just to be safe, she pushed the door open with her backside to keep her hands clean. Thomas was sitting where she had left him. "Are you off the phone already?"

"No, I didn't have time. I started to leave, but then I was notified that Peter's in his room. I knew you wouldn't want to wait."

"Yeah, let's go. Do you have the room number?" Adrenaline surged through Anne's body making all signs of an ill stomach vanish as she rushed to the elevators down the hall.

Thomas sprinted to catch up with her. "We need to go to the third floor, room 303." Except for Anne thumbing her nails on the elevator door, they traveled in silence to Peter's room. Anne slowed as she entered his room; she had braced herself to see all sorts of tubes and machines. She was surprised to see Peter looking normal, like he was sleeping except for one IV in his left arm.

Anne made her way to Peter's side. She picked up his right hand and squeezed. She paused only for a moment to thank God for her son's life. Anne spoke to Peter in a low, even tone, "Hi, honey. I'm so glad to see you. You look great . . . considering."

Thomas glared at Anne, "Don't say considering . . . it sounds sad."

"I don't know what to say." Anne chewed lip. "Can you hear us?" she tried again. Peter made no indication he heard them. Anne continued, "I love you. Your dad and I are both here, and we love you so much."

Thomas interrupted, "Anne, you sound so sad. Let's talk about something happy."

"What am I supposed to talk about then?"

Thomas paused for a moment, "Peter, your mom and I were talking about the time she threw up all over herself at the grocery store."

Anne picked up on her memory. "Yeah, it was the day I picked you up from school after the tuna incident." Still sedated with medication, Peter was unable to indicate he understood what they were saying. However, he did hear them and he did remember that day. He also recalled how they had worked out a deal with the school for him not to have to be in the same room as tuna ever again.

* * *

It had been part of Peter's infamous kindergarten year, and Peter could do no right as far as the school was concerned. Thomas issued Mrs. Krieg a medical prescription for a tuna substitute to get around the school policy. His formal excuse read something like, *Peter was at risk for malnourishment if he was not offered a substitute in place of tuna because of his medically-diagnosed food aversion.*

Anne had arranged with the school for Peter to bring a bag lunch on tuna days, but he couldn't eat it in the lunchroom because that violated federal regulations of having competition with the hot lunch program. Peter had to take the bag lunch to the library as that was the only room that staffed a teacher over lunch, because it was concurrently used as the detention room.

A couple weeks after the tuna exemption was implemented, the fish was back on the menu, and Peter was once again prepared with a bag lunch. Traumatized from the last bag-lunch incident, Peter was petrified of having someone throw it away again, so he didn't let his lunch bag out of his site. The only class he had before lunch was music, so instead of leaving his lunch bag in the classroom, he carried it with him. Once inside the music room, he tucked it under his seat.

That day, they sang "Frosty the Snowman" and Peter was the loudest one. He loved the sound of his voice. Peter adored music class because this was the only place he was told to let his voice be heard. Everywhere else he went, people told him to be quiet. In addition to getting to make lots of sound, his music teacher, Mrs. Polly was sweet, and she always had a smile on her face.

The class was preparing for the annual Christmas concert in a couple of weeks. Peter couldn't stop thinking about being on stage and singing so loudly everyone in the school could hear him. The best part – Mrs. Polly had picked two students, one boy and one girl, for a solo, and he got the boy part! Mrs. Polly hand-selected "Away in the Manger" for Peter to sing, because it was perfect for a little soprano voice. *I get to sing into a real microphone and it's going to awesome!*

The class went fast, and before he knew it, they were being asked to line up for lunch. Everyone was standing up except Peter, because

Mrs. Polly asked him to wait for a couple seconds while she grabbed some learning materials for his solo.

"I'm hurrying to find it. I had it just a second ago. Oh wait. Here it is," Mrs. Polly called from the supply closet. She hustled over to where Peter was standing and presented a sheet and a CD to him. "Just have your mom help you with the lyrics until you know them by heart. Next week, you and I can find some time, maybe during recess, to sit down at the piano and practice the song. Oh, and there's a recording on the CD you can listen to, so you can hear it sung."

Peter didn't say anything, but he thought, *I'm going to practice every day. My mom's going to be so proud of me when she sees me on stage; the whole school will see that I'm someone special.*

"You better hurry and catch up to the class or you'll miss lunch," Mrs. Polly interrupted Peter's daydream. Peter looked up and saw the last student had filed out of the class and the door was shutting behind them.

"I'm not going with them anyway. I have my own lunch. I hate tuna." He stuck out his tongue in a pretend gag. "I have to take this to the detention room." He grabbed his bag lunch and started over to the exit door.

"You got detention?"

"No, but I'm not allowed in the lunchroom with a bag lunch and that's the only other room where a teacher's working during lunch."

Mrs. Polly studied his sad face. "You know Peter; I have a bag lunch too. I was going to eat it now in my classroom. If you want to eat with me, we can work on your solo now. I can call down to your teacher and get it approved." Peter's face lit up, and without hesitation, he nodded a big "Yes". *Mrs. Polly's the nicest person in this school. I'm so lucky I get to spend my lunch with her.*

"Okay, wait here while I make my calls, and I need to grab my lunch too. It's in the fridge in the teachers' lounge across the hall.

Can I treat you to a cold juice or something from the machine in there?"

Peter's heart was bursting. *Ah man, I bet the teacher's lounge has the best juice! But, if I drank two juices, I might have an accident, so I better not.* He shook his head and said, "No thanks." Mrs. Polly left the room for a few seconds and Peter, who could never sit still, looked down at the piano keys.

His fingers were usually tight. Being left handed, the fingers on that hand were more limber as they got used more. He stuck out his left index finger to push one key all the way down. He waited as he absorbed the sound. *That sounds like the higher-pitched key Mrs. Polly just played.* He wanted more.

With his index finger, he pressed the next key and the next, and listened to them one at a time. *I think these keys here are pretty much the keys she used for "Frosty the Snowman".* He plucked out the tune, trying to make it sound the same. When he messed up, he started over until he found the right rhythm. *Aha! I got it. That's it!* Deep in thought with his tongue hanging out the left side of his mouth in thinking-cap mode, he finished the song. He even clapped for himself. *That's awesome! I did it!* He looked around to find his missing teacher, and he was startled to see she was standing beside him.

"Oh hi. You scared me," he said and then giggled nervously.

"I was listening to you play."

Peter folded his bottom lip in in fright and then said, "I'm sorry. I didn't mean to play. I mean, I should have asked. I was sitting here and had that song in my head." Peter was accustomed to having everyone in his world upset with him, so he was always on auto-apology mode.

"You're not in trouble. I liked it. I didn't know you played piano. Who gives you lessons?" Mrs. Polly bit into a baby carrot while she held the bag with the opposite hand and plopped down next to Peter on the bench.

"I don't play the piano. I just sat here."

Mrs. Polly furrowed her eyebrows. "Peter, I heard you play just now. It was perfect. Who taught you that? Does your mom or dad play?"

"No, I never played. I just heard the song because you played it. I pushed the keys and they sounded like the right ones," Peter defended.

Mrs. Polly smiled in a disbelieving way. "You did a nice job. Let's work on your solo. I'll play it on the piano first, and then we can sing it together. Don't worry if you don't get it right away as this is just practice." She played and sang. Peter loved the song and the piano, and Mrs. Polly had such a pretty voice.

Peter quickly learned the correct pitch and words. They sang, and played and ate their lunch in-between verses. Peter had a blast. "Oh, that's the first bell Peter, you'd better get your stuff and head back to class," Mrs. Polly urged him at the sound of buzzing.

"I go on the second bell, which is in three more minutes. Can I try the piano part before I go?" Peter asked with his cheeks turning pink.

Mrs. Polly turned her head to the side in surprise. "Sure." She moved her body over to the side of the bench. Peter centered himself on the keys he needed, and then plucked out the exact chords to "Away in the Manger". When he was finished, he lifted his head and proclaimed, "I watched you this time, so it was easier to find the keys."

Mrs. Polly swallowed. She saw him watch her play and now he played it almost as well as she did. "That was beautiful Peter." By now, she was on to his teasing.

"Can we have lunch next week too?" Peter asked.

"Sure, we can try to work on this solo again. I'll let you know Monday what day works for me."

"Cool!" Peter said, excited as he grabbed his garbage and headed out the door. *This was the best day!*

Five

ANNE

Despite the air-conditioning unit puttering away under the window, Peter's hospital room was muggy from the changing weather outside. Anne had held Peter's hand in silence for hours while she stared at his closed eyelids. *I really need you to be okay. I need you to be strong. . .* Her thoughts were interrupted by the sound of Paul, Tane, and Shiloh walking into the room. They stood back to watch their brother lying in his hospital bed.

"It's fine boys. Come on in," Thomas said. "He's going to be okay. He's just sedated."

"Can he hear us?" Shiloh asked as he shifted awkwardly from one foot to the other.

"I don't know," Thomas said. Turning to Anne, he said, "I asked the boys to come up to visit now because you need to take a break. We both do. You've been up all night. We should go home to rest."

Anne arched her eyebrows. "I don't want to leave before Peter wakes up. I'm going to stay the night again."

"I sort of thought you would say that so I had Shiloh pack you a bag. You might as well shower here since we're paying for the room." As Thomas spoke, Shiloh slid a backpack off his shoulder and placed it next to his mom.

"I brought you some clean clothes. You need them." Shiloh wrinkled his noise to tease Anne, who almost smiled. Shiloh was Anne's second biggest momma's boy, after Peter. She swore, after raising Peter, she was done having kids, but now looking at her son, Shiloh, she couldn't imagine what she would do without him.

Shiloh was short for his age and the quietest of all the Arnold boys. Thomas referred to Shiloh as an 'easy keeper', a term they used on Thomas's childhood ranch to label a horse that was low maintenance. Shiloh had dark hair like Tane and Paul. Currently, he was going through the stage where he refused haircuts. The longer his hair grew out, the wavier it got and it looked like a surfer haircut.

Anne grabbed Shiloh's bag, and then with her free hand, she reached for his extended hand and squeezed. "Thank you, bud." *I don't want to go home, but a shower does sound awesome.* Anne stood up and went into the adjacent bathroom. *I have the best children, but, right now, I'm so proud of Shiloh.* Anne remembered how crazy life was when he was added to her family.

● ● ●

It was nearly a dozen years ago, and Anne was weeks out from her due date with Shiloh. She was not ready for another addition yet. Peter's kindergarten-adjustment issues had consumed all her time, and she had little energy to even dig out the old baby cloths and crib. She needed to replenish consumable supplies like: diapers, wipes, and diaper cream. Her need to shop worked out well because Thomas had taken the day off to give her a break and to attend parent-teacher conferences.

She shopped at her favorite boutiques until she realized she had only about thirty minutes to get to the school. She felt uneasy about the meeting but she knew Thomas would be able to handle any uncomfortable conversation. Marie was going to babysit her brothers, and Anne planned to meet Thomas at the school to save on commuting time.

Although it was a trying time for her, pregnancy was always sweet because she was the only one who got to know the baby in such an intimate way. It wasn't going to be long before everyone else would know the baby too. Anne rubbed her belly, *almost time for everyone to meet you.* She made her final purchases, loaded them into the van, and drove to the school.

Anne and Thomas had been invited to come a half hour before regular conferences for a meeting with Peter's teachers along with the principal. They were not sure how many parents got this special privilege, but it was discouraging. They sat at a long table in the principal's office with the gym teacher, music teacher, and his classroom teacher. Anne was jittery as she didn't know what to expect. Thomas looked cool and was even making jokes about having to be in the principal's office.

"Well, let's dive right into our agenda for tonight. We don't have a lot of time as we have a packed schedule," Mrs. Krieg said after introductions. "We all know of the previous discussions and accommodations we've made for Peter. We know he has had trouble adjusting and transitioning and as experienced educators, we're concerned. We recommend Peter be evaluated for some medical support. Yes, we know you're a physician," she nodded at Thomas, "but we have valid concerns. Where are you guys in this process?"

Thomas leaned forward to retrieve a white ballpoint pen from the center of the conference table. "I see Peter every day and if I felt there were something out there that could help him pharmaceutically, then I would be the first to recommend it. He's highly sensitive. It makes him see the world in a little distorted way. His senses are always in overdrive; he gets overwhelmed easier. It makes things hard for him but it's not a disease." Thomas bounced the end of the pen on the table as he held it with his thumb and index finger. Anne watched the pen bounce up and down, refusing to make eye contact with Mrs. Krieg.

Mrs. Krieg was not easily convinced. "We have a school psychiatrist who is waiting to see Peter. I know you're in the clinic working with families, but this isn't your specialty. We're just asking for an evaluation and we need a parent's signed permission slip."

"I appreciate your interest in Peter, but we'll handle the medical issues at home," Thomas said. He turned to the gym teacher, Mr. Logan. "How's Peter hitting those curve balls?"

Mr. Logan spoke, "No curve balls yet." He laughed and continued, "Peter's busy, but he likes to work through things and get them right. He does get upset if things aren't his way. He has a hard time with transitions," Mr. Logan paused and looked towards Mrs. Krieg.

Anne watched Mr. Logan stare at Mrs. Krieg and she felt like he was being coached on what to say. "He loves your class," Thomas said as he looked at Mrs. Polly.

Mrs. Polly's eyes darted towards Mrs. Krieg and then back to Thomas, "I adore Peter. He sings the loudest. He's the busiest. He's ecstatic about his solo next week. I was working with him today, and he's catching on quickly." She paused, and then smiled, "He does like to tease, though. He played the piano while we were singing, and he insisted he never took lessons." Mrs. Polly shook her head and shrugged with a half-smile. "He's a story teller."

"He doesn't take lessons," Anne said.

"Oh, he got lessons from somewhere because he plays perfect."

"No, I've never left him anywhere with a piano. He never went to preschool or anywhere until he started school here. He's never had lessons," Anne defended.

"I don't know, Anne, you should ask him to play. He tells me he's never had lessons, but he can play. You don't just sit down at the piano and play like that."

"Well, we're not here to talk about piano lessons," Mrs. Krieg interrupted. "We need to also address Peter's absences. He has already missed the maximum amount of time allowed to pass for the year. In normal situations, we would hold him back, but there's a caveat in kindergarten. Right now, he's only doing the half-day in the afternoon. As you know, we added full days of kindergarten last year. In the morning, we do enrichment. It's up to the parents to decide if they want to enroll their kids in full days, but for Peter, I would suggest you start bringing him in for the whole day. We could use it to make up some time."

"He can barely make it through a half day, how's he gonna to make it through a full day?" Anne asked.

"Maybe he'll do better in the mornings. His brain will be fresh and rested. I don't know what else to do – short of holding him back – but we're only halfway through the year."

Anne looked to Thomas, who nodded back at her. "We can try it," she said.

"Great, I can let Val know to email you the papers to enroll in our enrichment program. We can start first thing Monday. Just drop him off with the rest of the kids." She pushed a paper at Anne, "Here's the form I need signed and returned for the medical evaluation. Please take it home to review it. And, I'm afraid this is all the time we have for this meeting, especially since we are unable to form a unified consensus about the evaluation," Mrs. Krieg said. She got up from her chair, walked to the door, and stood next to it, waiting to escort everyone out.

Anne wanted to finish her conversation with Mrs. Polly, but this wasn't a good time. She would talk to Peter when she got home. *How silly Mrs. Polly was, insisting Peter could play piano.*

They drove home in the separate cars they arrived in, but once home, Anne hopped into the passenger side of Thomas's truck.

Thomas reached for her hand to help her up into the seat. "What are you thinking?" He asked as he pulled her under his arm in a side snuggle. "Are you angry?"

"No, I knew it was coming. I think something has changed with Mrs. Krieg though, because she used to be so supportive. Just a few weeks ago, she was playing dinosaurs on the floor with Peter. Tonight, she was practically growling."

"It did sound like she was growling. Didn't it? Maybe that's her dinosaur growl?" Thomas tried to imitate it as best he could. They both laughed.

Anne sighed, "What are we going to do?"

"We're going to go inside and make dinner. We can be thankful for this problem because it could be worse, but I'm going to forget about that meeting." Thomas took Mrs. Krieg's form that Anne was holding and wadded it up into a ball.

"I agree," Anne said as she turned to get out of the vehicle.

Thomas climbed out of his truck and something caught his eye. The living-room light was on, the curtain was open, and you could see right into the room. Thomas wasn't looking into the room, though. He was stuck on the window. One of the panels in the bay window was broken. He flew up the walkway, and sure enough, as he walked his feet crunched shattered glass all over the ground. Anne was right behind him as she saw it too. "What the . . .," Thomas said.

He flung the front door wide open and yelled, "Kids get out here! Where's my window?"

Marie came out from the kitchen with Peter under her arm. Her hair was ratted in the back like she had been wrestling and her eyes were as wide as pancakes, "Thank Goodness your home. I'm not ever babysitting again!"

"We're painting with thumbs, mom," Peter said as he held up his blue and green thumbs.

Thomas yelled again, "Boys get out here. Marie where are your brothers?"

Marie looked down. "They left after they smashed the window."

"Huh? They did this?" Thomas asked. "Paul and Tane did this?"

"Yeah, they were wrestling and fell on the floor lamp, and it just punched the window right out. I told them you would kill them when you got home. They didn't want to get into trouble, so they ran away," Marie said.

"What do you mean, they ran away? Are they outback?" Thomas walked to the back door in five giant steps, threw it open, and called for the boys, but he heard no reply. "Where are they?" He asked Marie again as he walked back through the front of the house.

"I told you; they left. They ran away," Marie replied.

"Where did they go?" Thomas asked, but his voice was booming so loud, it discouraged Marie from answering him.

"Oh great. Where do you think they went?" It's getting so cold and dark out," Anne said as she looked out the window.

"I don't know. They're jerks, and they were picking on Peter. He was getting upset, so I told them to find something to do. They wrestled each other, broke the window, and then they left. We're glad they are gone. Much quieter," Marie said. Peter giggled holding his thumbs up again.

"You shouldn't have let them leave by themselves, something could happen. How long have they been gone?" Anne asked.

"An hour, maybe?" Marie nervously pulled her lip with fingers.

Annoyed, Thomas said, "Marie, you watch Peter. Don't leave the house. You call me if you see them. Hear me?"

"Yes, Sir."

"Anne, you go ask the neighbors," he paused as he saw her pregnant silhouette. He couldn't have her running around at night.

"Wait, you take the van and check the park. I'll go on foot and check with the neighbors. They're probably around the block somewhere."

Anne was already out the door, calling people. As she pulled the van up next to the sidewalk that surrounded the park, she could see it was obviously vacant. Her nerves made her shaky and her back was aching. *This is NOT how I wanted my night to end.* She drove on; the neighborhood seemed quiet.

Anne texted Thomas, "Any luck? Not at the park. Headed to school now."

Thomas texted back, "No luck with neighbors. I'll meet you at school."

Thomas met Anne outside the school, and they scavenged the playground. The sky was dark, and the time was approaching 7:00 p.m. They tried the front doors to the school, and Thomas looked at Anne in surprise when they opened, but then they both said out loud at the same time, "Conferences!"

The hall was dotted with a few conference stragglers. Thomas motioned to the janitor who was busy vacuuming the front entry-way, "Hey Arney, have you seen Paul or Tane tonight?"

"No, but I've been waxing the floor in the gym. You can check with Val."

"Thanks," Anne and Thomas both chimed at the same time. They raced to the front office.

"Val, have you seen Paul or Tane?" Anne blurted out when she saw Valerie.

Valerie looked up, adjusted her round, wire glasses up higher onto her nose, and said, "I don't think so. It's been mostly parents tonight without kids. Didn't you guys just leave here?"

Thomas spoke, "Yeah, but the boys are missing. We left them with Marie, and they told her they were running away."

"Well, let me make an announcement to see if they are here or if anyone has seen them." She slid her chair over to the intercom microphone and paged the boys. After waiting awhile with nobody buzzing back, Thomas said, "We'd better get going, Anne."

Anne looked at Val, "Do you have any ideas where an eight and a nine-year-old would run away to? They were on foot."

"Have you tried the mall, or maybe a movie?"

"No, I didn't think they would go all the way up there, but we can check."

"All the other doors are locked and people have to leave out this door. I can watch for them," Valerie said.

"Thank you," Anne said. Her back hurt so badly, she could barely stand still. They walked out together into the cool, night air; Anne couldn't help but be reminded it was supposed to get down into the thirties. For a Minnesota December, thirty degrees was mild, but Anne didn't want to be out running around in it, and it wasn't safe for her boys to be out either.

"Burr," Thomas muttered as he fumbled with the van key. "We really need to upgrade to one of those new vans with electronic, remote locks." He looked at his wife. She was pasty white, standing by the passenger side of the van.

"Tom," Anne said as she stared out into the sky. Her voice was so weak, it was almost iridescent and it sent chills down Thomas's spine. "You alright?" He asked. She didn't move. She never called him "Tom" either, which alarmed him as he rushed over to her side of the van where she stood clenching the van door with white knuckles.

As Thomas turned the bend around the corner he saw it; the water. Anne's feet were soaked and centered in a water puddle. "Your water broke."

Anne cut him off as she regained composure and tried to climb into the van. "I'm fine. Contractions haven't started yet; let's go look for the boys."

"Anne, you need to go into the hospital. You shouldn't be on your feet until we know the baby's head's engaged." Anne didn't hear Thomas.

"I can't go to the hospital until I know my boys are safe," Anne said. "Get in the van. Let's go to the mall. Contractions haven't started yet, and it could take hours."

"I'm calling Dr. Larry to meet us at the hospital." Thomas slid into the driver's seat.

"You can tell him it will be a while before I get there because I'm not going there with my boys out missing." Anne motioned for Thomas to start driving, "Lets ge eeet ooh!" Anne screamed as she grabbed her back.

"That's a contraction. You're in labor, Anne. It's time to go in now," Thomas said sternly as he reversed the van swiftly.

"It was a spasm! I'm not in labor. Go to the mall!" Anne screamed. Thomas was not listening as he was on the phone with her doctor. He stopped at the stop sign where he needed to turn left to go to the mall, instead he went straight in the direction of the hospital. Anne was furious. *I know my own body and it's not time*! She leaned over to the steering wheel, grabbed it, jerking it left. "I said, let's go to the mall!"

Thomas gripped the wheel tight for control of the van. "You're going to get us killed, Anne! Sit back."

"I can't go yet. I have to know my kids safe. What if something happens? I have to find them first." Anne sobbed so hard that she lost her strength and Thomas could push her hand back off the wheel and she didn't even notice. "Thomas, I can't have a baby if I'm missing two of my other babies," she wailed.

"We'll find them. They're not missing. We just don't know where they are yet. They have only been gone a few hours. Call your sister and tell her to meet you at the hospital. I'll find them.

Anne called her sister. Thomas called Marie and got an update – no word from the boys. Thomas told Marie to get Peter dressed, grab mom's hospital bag, and wait by the door. It was getting too late for them to stay by themselves. Marie would go to the hospital with Anne, and Peter would help him look for the boys.

"Is the baby coming?" Marie's squealed.

"It looks like it won't be long. Be ready. Oh, and put a note on the door if the boys come back to call us. Tell them it's urgent." He hated to leave the house empty with the boys gone but he couldn't leave the other kids by themselves this late. He decided to call the neighbor, Janice, and ask her to watch for the boys too. After that call, he looked at Anne and she was quiet. She was gazing past the window, looking scared to death; Thomas drove the van faster.

"Thomas, I think we need to go look at the mall. They have that big arcade the boys love. I bet they're there."

"Anne, I'll look as soon as I drop you off."

"Well, if you're not going to take me then I'll do it myself!" Anne said as she opened the van door and half jumped, half fell out onto the sidewalk. She turned around, in the direction of the mall and waddled her way toward it.

"You turkey!" Thomas jerked the steering wheel, pulling it over so he could jump out after her. "Pregnancy hormones," he muttered under his breath. "Anne, this is dangerous! You know you can't walk that far in labor."

"Walking's good for labor."

"Yeah, if you want to have this baby on the sidewalk, but your water isn't intact. You know you're being foolish."

She continued to waddle down the street. "I can't have my babies missing."

"What can I do to get you to go to the hospital?"

"You can get my babies. Oh, oh! Oh, man!" Anne grabbed her

back. Her contractions were getting closer. Thomas reached for Anne's arms and held them tightly so she wouldn't escape.

"Let me go," Anne screamed and twisted trying to escape his hold.

"No," he said as he squirmed to keep her still.

"You're crazy!" Anne wiggled and pulled so hard trying to escape that she fell to the ground. Thomas came with her – still holding her arms locked with one arm. On the ground, Anne felt the cold earth beneath her, reminding her of the boys outside. *They must be getting cold.*

Thomas broke her thoughts by saying, "Let me handle this. You go to the hospital and worry about this baby." He placed his hand on her belly and continued, "I'll find our boys. We're wasting time."

Anne was scared to death. Tane and Paul had never tried anything like this before tonight. She needed them found. "Okay I will go, but you promise you'll find them quickly."

"Let's go," Thomas said, holding his hand out to help Anne off the ground. They drove in silence to pick up Marie and Peter. Marie had no news from the boys and she looked guilty.

"I'm sorry mom. I didn't know they would actually leave and be gone this long," Marie said.

"You should have called me right away, Marie," Anne said. Her contractions were getting closer together and harder; she didn't have words of comfort to offer Marie. She knew she had just a few hours before this baby needed to be born, and she hoped everything would be back to normal by then. She didn't want Thomas to miss the birth, but she wasn't going to let him come back without her Tane and Paul.

Thomas helped Anne into a wheel chair outside the hospital where Anne's sister, Maggie, was waiting to receive her. Together, Maggie and Marie wheeled Anne through the hospital doors. Anne watched her husband drive away.

Six

THOMAS

After Thomas had dropped Anne and Marie off at the hospital, Thomas drove around in search without a plan. He tried to brainstorm by interviewing Peter again. "What did the boys say before they left?"

"They didn't want to get in trouble. They were gonna live in the woods."

"Woods?" Thomas drummed his fingers on the steering wheel as he drove. *Minnesota has trees, but there really aren't woods anywhere in town.* He checked the clock on the dash, it read almost 9:00 p.m., and the temperature was dropping rapidly. *They've been gone over three hours. They've got to be getting hungry . . . and cold.*

"Maybe they stopped home?" he asked Peter, but it was more to himself. He dialed Janice's number on his cell phone. "Hey Janice, would you do me a favor and go sit at the house so you can watch for the boys?" He ran his hand through his dark hair and let his fingers linger on top of his head to knead his scalp easing the tension.

"I suppose I can do that. You still don't have any word from them?" she asked.

"Nope, I'm sort of confused as where else to look. We've been everywhere within walking distance."

"Well, I'm sure it won't be long now. Usually, this running-away game is fun until you get hungry."

"I'm hoping that's the case this time too." Thomas checked the rearview mirror to see that Peter eyelids were starting to droop. "Call me if you see them please. I better pay attention here."

"Will do, bye," Janice said.

"Thank you. Bye."

Thomas coasted around the neighborhood with his eyes peeled for clues. The winter sky was clouded without light to illuminate his search. He checked some gas stations for the boys, but there was no sign of them. He drove faster now, and he started to check fast-food restaurants, and even hotel lobbies, on the way to the mall. *They must be somewhere inside because it's so cold out.*

Thomas pulled the van into an almost empty parking lot at the mall. "Come on Peter. Let's check one more place." Peter obliged and slid out of his seat. He held Thomas's hand as they darted into the mall entrance straight into the piercing wind.

"It burns," Peter said.

"I know bud, run!" Thomas tucked his chin down into the collar of his jacket.

"I can't see," Peter said as the wind irritated his eyes to the point of tears. Thomas reached down, pulled Peter up to carry him, and ran faster. Once inside, Thomas placed Peter on the ground.

"Ah man, the burr willies are out tonight." Thomas rubbed his hands. *I'm glad Anne doesn't know how cold it's now.* "Here, let's go this way to the janitor's office." Thomas led Peter through the entryway.

They found the janitor driving a floor scrubber by the food court. He shut off the machine when he saw Thomas waving. "Excuse me, I'm sorry to bother you, but I was hoping you could do me favor?" Thomas implored.

"I can try," he said.

"I'm looking for my two boys. Can you make an announcement over the intercom?" Peter clung to Thomas's leg, wiggling so much it almost pulled Thomas off balance. He glared at Peter. *Can't you stand still for ONE minute?*

"I can do that, just wait here. I'll call them to the food court."

"Thank you, Sir. I appreciate it," Thomas said as the man left. Peter leaned into Thomas's leg hard. Thomas stepped back to balance himself. "Knock it off, Peter!" Thomas grabbed Peter's arm, pulling him into a standing position. "Can you stand still?" Peter folded his chin down and stood straight for two seconds. Then, he traced the tile lines on the floor with one foot. *How does Anne get anything done with Peter? I'm going to lose it.*

An announcement came over the intercom and Thomas waited – nothing. A few moments passed, the announcement repeated, and still nothing. The janitor came back and shrugged. Thomas concluded the mall was a dead end and left.

Back into the van, Thomas and Peter continued their search, driving back towards home again. "I'm tired, dad. I want to go home," Peter said.

"I know bud. We can't go home until we find your brothers."

"I want mom."

"Mom's at the hospital. You can't go there." Thomas stopped at a red light and turned back to look at Peter; his eyes were rubbed red underneath. "We have to look for your brothers." Peter grunted and rubbed his eyes again. The light turned green. Thomas could hear Peter quietly protesting as he drove, but eventually it got less and then Peter was asleep.

Thomas tapped his fingers on the steering wheel. *Who can I call? Where would they be?* His phone beeped notifying him of a text. It was Anne.

"I'm 7 centimeters. Where are you?"

"Driving. I checked mall. Nothing."

"You better find them! And, hurry!!!!"

Thomas's head got even heavier as he threw the phone on the passenger seat. *I'm trying!* Thomas's phone rang. He rolled his eyes as he grabbed it, looking for Anne's number as he quickly turned the volume down. He checked Peter in the rearview mirror; he was still sleeping. The caller I.D. number was unrecognizable. *I don't know who this is, but I don't even care. It must be good news.*

"Hello."

"Yeah, Thomas?" the caller said.

"Yes, this is Thomas."

"Hey, this is Father Raymond."

Please don't be calling about medical advice. "Hi, how are you, Father?"

"I'm good. I was headed outside to plant my trees, and I noticed there were a little Tom Sawyer and Huck Finn camping out in my hills."

Thomas felt a huge surge of emotion flood his chest. "We've been looking for them. Tell me where they are, and I'll be there."

"They're up on the hill behind the church, but it's sort of hard to find them. Do you want to meet me up there?"

"Yeah, that would be great. I'll be there in five minutes." Thomas hung up the phone. He pushed his foot down hard on the gas pedal, accelerating the van to over 50 miles an hour in residential areas. Driving with his knees, he texted Anne, "Father Raymond called. He found the boys. I'm going to get them. Be there soon. Love you."

Barely three seconds later he got a text back that said, "Thank God and hurry!!!"

Thomas guided the van up the dirt path leading up the hill behind the church. The road stopped at the little cabin on the hill and he pulled his van into the clearing.

He spotted Father coming down the hill from a clearing in the trees. Thomas jumped out of his van to greet him. Father Raymond wore camouflage and carried a flashlight. *It's a little weird that Father's out running around the hills by himself in the middle of the night. He said he was planting trees . . . It's December. You can't plant trees in December. I guess whatever, I'm just grateful he found my boys.* He was about to run over to meet Father when he remembered Peter was asleep in the backseat.

Thomas looked into the window to check on Peter. His head had fallen all the way over to the side. A moist trail of drool glistened down his chin to confirm he was fully passed out. *If I wake him up, he'll be a bear, and it would be terrible to get him to calm down. It's freezing out, and I don't need him with his weak immune system traipsing all over the hills.* He motioned for Father to come all the way to the van. Father hustled over. "Peter's sleeping in the van. Anne's with Marie at the hospital; she's in labor. I didn't have anywhere to take him and I don't want to wake him; he was way overtired. Do you want to stay here by the van and I can go?"

"You might not see them. They're hiding pretty well. The only reason I found them is that I'm up here all the time, and I saw a few footsteps, so I followed them. It'll only take about ten minutes if we hurry. Maybe just lock the doors and I'll run back?"

Thomas was concerned about leaving Peter in the van, but he didn't really see another option. *He's sleeping. It'll be fast and then Father will be back.* "Okay. Let's run." Thomas nodded his head, and they were off.

Father Raymond was a younger priest in his thirties, so he could run at a good pace. They sprinted up the hill and around a bend in the trees. Father pointed to some little footprints, which were barely visible. The ground had been slightly moist from melted snow in a couple low areas, and mud captured the footprints when it refroze. They followed the prints through another clearing, which left the main path.

Slowing down, Father said in whisper, "I don't want to run up on them, because they'll hear us and they might run off scared." Thomas could then see the soft glow of light, and as they took another couple of steps forward he saw some shadows. *Never in a million years would I approach those shadows if I didn't know it was Paul and Tane.*

They walked around another evergreen tree and Thomas could see their faces. The boys must have heard steps and both looked up at the same time. They had the exact same expression on their faces, a wide-open mouth and frozen eye contact with Thomas.

"Dad!" Tane called.

"Dad! You scared the crud out of me!" Paul screamed as he had jumped to his feet and grabbed a stick, ready to pounce on a predator. "What are you doing here?"

"I came to take you home. Father saw you out here and called me. Thank God! Are you trying to get killed? Who knows what's hiding out here?" Thomas wanted to say so much more, but he just didn't have time for it.

"We're camping out here. We're not going home," Tane said as he shinned a flashlight directly at Thomas, blinding him.

Thomas stepped out of the light. "Yeah you are. You need to get up and out of here fast because your mom's in labor – about to have the baby. I need to get to her. I don't have time for games. Peter's sleeping in the car . . ." his voice trailed off. "Peter!" He repeated as he looked at Father. He had forgotten already.

Father nodded, "I'll go back if you can find your way?"

"We will," Thomas said, and Father ran back down the path. Thomas looked around and saw the boys had flashlights, sleeping bags, and what looked like a bag of food. "Where did you get all this stuff?"

"We grabbed it out of the garage from the camping stuff before we left," Tane said. He had a proud smirk on his face like he thought it was funny.

"Pick it up! We don't have any time to spare. Let's go!" Thomas urged as he grabbed a sleeping bag, rolled it up, and threw it under his arm. He motioned for the boys to gather their stuff. He needed them to move. "Hurry!"

Paul and Tane were completely obedient; they collected their supplies while Thomas tried to recover the last of his patience. *Paul and Tane are good boys, but they could have picked a better day to pull this stunt. Any other day, this might have been funny, but not now,* Thomas had one thing on his mind – Anne.

He was sweating cannonballs by the time he got to the hospital. He ordered the boys out of the van. It was a good thing Thomas was a doctor at the hospital because he didn't stop at the front for registration or any kind of permission. He knew where the delivery room was located, and he plowed over everything in his path to get to Anne. The hospital staff moved to clear a path for him as he blazed through. The boys tried their best to keep up, but all three were way overtired and in terrible moods, so they trailed behind.

As they approached the delivery room, they saw Marie sitting outside of it with her back against the wall. She wore her music headphones to block out the screaming. When she saw her family coming, she took out her ear buds. "Dad! Hurry! The baby's here! Mom made me come out here because the baby's here!" She stood, and jumped up and down as she motioned for them to hurry.

Thomas sprinted the last few steps as he called to the boys to stay in the hall with Marie. He blasted through the doors. All Thomas saw, once inside the room, was Anne's doctor reaching down to pull the baby out of Anne. It was a him! Thomas burst into tears as he ran to Anne's bedside. Anne reached for her new son and placed him on her chest. Relief finally grazed over Anne's face. In a calm voice, Thomas said, "The boys are here. All four of them."

Anne looked down at the little miracle in her hands, smiling through her tears, "All my boys are here now." They embraced as a new family for the first time. "All moments in life are precious, but beginnings are the sweetest ones," Anne said as she kissed the top of Shiloh's peach-fuzz head.

Seven

PETER

"All moments in life are precious, but beginnings are the sweetest ones," Thomas whispered to Peter. He was still medically sedated, but he looked like a sleeping child. "Do you know that's what your mom said to each one of you kids when you were born?" Thomas waited for a sign that Peter heard him. There was no sign.

Thomas continued, "I was thinking about that night you and I drove all over looking for Paul and Tane. We made a pretty good team that night. Didn't we?" Thomas squeezed Peter's hand. "Do you remember that night? It was the night Shiloh was born. I'll never forget that night as long as I live." He sighed heavily still unable to tell if Peter could hear him.

Peter heard him all right. *I know the night you're talking about. I'll never forget it! I still have nightmare about it.*

◦ ◦ ◦

Peter remembered how he had woken up to find himself in the van, sitting in his car seat – alone. *It's cold in here.* He opened his eyes, *its dark in here and dad's gone.* Frightened, he unsnapped his seatbelt to climb down from his seat, and slid through the center isle of the van into the driver's seat. He looked out of the windshield where he had a front-row seat to where they were parked, *the Goat Woman's house!*

Immediately, he collapsed onto the floor to hide under the dash; he was instantly dizzy, and his chest was tight. After pausing a moment, he rose slowly to peek over the dash again. *There it is, and nobody's here.* The house looked worse up close. Paint was chipped off the wood siding, giving the cabin an abandoned farmhouse look. The roof hung low to cover the front porch, creating shadows that added to the creepiness. An almost transparent, white, linen curtain hung over a window above the deck where a single, yellow glow illuminated the interior of the house.

Peter gulped out loud. *The Goat Woman has dad! He's in there. She has him!* Visions of his dad being tied up and tortured flashed through his mind. *Oh no! What am I going to do? I need to call mom.* Peter looked around; the cell phone was gone. *It must be with dad.*

His heart jumped around in his chest so fast he became dizzy again. Then, he had another thought and it almost crippled him. *I'm stuck here! Dad's gone, and I'm here. I have to get out! There are no keys! Not that I know how to drive a van, but how hard could it be really.* He looked out the back window and saw the long, dirt road down the hill. *I'm gonna have to run down that hill.* He looked at his leg braces stabilizing his ankles. *My legs don't work well for running, but I have to try.*

He pulled the door handle while he kept one eye fixed on the cabin; he was thinking and reacting fast. *I can't stay here another minute or I might be found. I'm going to jump out, run to the church, and go find Father Raymond to call mom.* Peter's breath was shallow and rapid. He watched the house while he tried to catch his breath.

Then, he had another thought; *I can't leave dad in there.* His eyes went back to the window with the light. *Maybe I can peek in there to see him?* He swallowed hard. There was a lump in his throat he had never felt before. He loved his dad, and his mom was going to have a baby tonight, and she needed his dad. He swallowed again. The lump was blocking his airway.

From somewhere deep inside of him that he never knew was there, he felt a strange calmness come over him. He knew what he had to do . . . so much so that he even said out loud, "A man has to do, what a man has to do."

He took another deep breath and jumped out of the van. Landing on the tips of his toes, he inched forward, careful to not make a sound. He had seen a show on TV where detectives walked around like this when they didn't want to be seen. *I'm gonna peep in the window for a second. If I don't see anything, I'll race down the hill.* He didn't know what he was going to do if he saw his dad. His mind wasn't thinking that far ahead yet.

Very slowly, one toe at a time, he crept towards the house. Peter held his chest with one hand in an effort to control his heartbeat. He thought it was ready to launch out of his chest. He visualized his heart flying out of his chest so far it knocked out the Goat Woman, allowing him time to free his dad.

He sneaked up to the bottom step of the deck and perched to let his eyes scope the place out. There was still no sign of anyone. *Up the steps, over to the window, look in, turn and run,* he planned. Repeating his plan quietly in his head about ten times, Peter tried to get the courage to actually do it. *Another deep breath and here I go.*

Deep breath in. Deep breath out, and he was off. Up one step, then the next, looking both ways for clearance and there was nothing. Peter glanced forward and there was nothing. He leaped towards the window. He landed on his feet with his knees bent and his face was pointed down like a frog landing on a lily pad. *Oh man! I'm on the deck of the Goat Woman's house! Wait until Tane and Paul hear this! Oh wait. They're missing. Oh no! I know why dad drove here! The Goat*

Woman had Paul and Tane, and Dad came here to get them, but he was captured too! They're all in there!

Nervous sweat poured down Peter's back despite the fact that it was freezing outside. *The nasty Goat Woman has my whole family! I must save them.* Frantic now, he knew what he had to do. Ever so slowly, he peered into the window.

The curtain made visibility difficult, but it was sheer enough he could see through it when he pressed his face all the way against the window. The room was lite from a roaring fire in the stone fireplace on the wall. He saw a kitchen table with some chairs. Three wooden shoe, box-size chests were laid out on the counter. He ducked down to catch his breath; he was relieved he didn't see anything too scary, but he wasn't done. He needed another glimpse.

Timidly, he raised himself back up, so he could see again. *There she was!* The Goat woman was standing at the stove with her back towards the window. Her long, gray robe hung to the floor, concealing her goat hooves. *That's her alright.*

Something was now on the table. *She has red garbage bags and something else. . . cloth or paper. I need to get closer.* He inched up on his toes; his legs wobbled as they supported his weight. *It has to be cloth because paper wouldn't lay like that. Bed sheets with red stains. Blood! Oh no!* Peter gasped. *She has bloody sheets! She killed my dad and wrapped in him a sheet!*

The Goat Woman walked over to the pile of bed sheets. She lifted one corner of the pile and laid her hands down on something. She picked up the object by holding the sheet, with it still lying in the center. As she raised it off the table, she turned towards the side counter by the boxes. Peter had a direct view of the object. She lowered it into the box. *It's a bloody blob. I don't know what, but she killed something!*

Peter's stomach churned loudly. He fell to his knees; he couldn't stand anymore. His imagination was wild. *Were Paul or Tane in the sheets too? No, the pile wasn't big enough for bodies.* He was panting. *One more look, I have to know if my family's still alive.*

He stood tall as he could on his toes; he strained his eyes. He dug deep for courage as he tried to stretch his neck like a crane just a little higher, and then it happened. Directly in front of him on the other side of the window pane, he saw a pair of glowing, green eyes. They were looking directly into his. *It was the Goat Woman!* She saw him. She was making eye contact with him. *Those are greenest eyes I've ever seen,* and they had a deafening glow to them. Peter froze for a life-flashing moment before he felt a warm liquid oozing down his leg; he was peeing his pants.

"AH!" he shrieked. Adrenaline surged through his body as he jolted out of his frozen state of fear and sprang off the deck. *Dad, Tane and Paul were gonners, but I'm not going to join them!* Peter's leg braces clicked as he ran hard and fast. *Where am I going to go? The van's a dead end because there's no keys. Up in the hills or down to the church? The Goat Woman's probably fast on my tail.* He couldn't decide. He was running out towards the road, but didn't know if he was going to go up or down when all the sudden wham! He ran smack into someone. *The Goat Woman! She's in front of me. She flies! She must have flown out in front of me. I ran into the Goat Woman and she's huge!* She had to be over six-feet tall and solid. She grabbed him, pulling him into a chest hold, she pinned him into her grasp. He wiggled, he screamed, he cried. He couldn't get out. "I don't want to die!" he cried out.

"Peter! Peter! Calm down," she called. She had a deep masculine voice. *God, if I have to die, don't let it take long. I don't want to see her goat face. Or those eyes!*

He stopped fighting, closed his eyes, covered his head, and tried to crouch down, but couldn't free her grasp. He was ready to die. "Hurry up and do it!"

"Peter, it's Father Raymond. Calm down," the voice said. The embrace on Peter became softer and less constricting. Peter's heart surged. *It's Father Raymond.* He opened his eyes, and Father was there; he was alone. *What's he doing out here? The Goat woman would get both of us!* "Father, we have to run! We have to run back to the church! The Goat woman has my dad and brothers, and she's after me!" Peter spilled out as he grabbed Father's hand, yanking him down the hill.

"Peter, your dad and brothers are fine. They're just up the hill and will be here in a few seconds. Calm down."

Father could see that Peter was sickened by something. His pupils were dilated; he had worked up a sweat and was white as a ghost. "No Father, I saw her. I saw the Goat Woman." He pointed towards the cabin with a trembling hand. "We have to run! She's coming after me! I saw her and her blood! She has bloody stuff!" Peter cried, tugging at Father's arm.

"Peter, can you see your dad over there? There's your brothers." Father pointed to the top of the hill where the boys' flashlights could be seen.

Peter saw the lights and got quiet. He looked back to the house; he saw no one coming after him. *It looks like my dad will be here in a little bit. He has keys and can drive the van away. That's the fastest way to get out of here, but I don't want to wait outside.* "I'm waiting in the van," he told Father.

Peter climbed back into the van, locking the door behind him. He bounced his gaze between the cabin door and the light beams descending on the hill towards him. He tapped his foot in the air to help calm his anxiety. All he wanted to do was get away from here. A couple minutes later, his dad was outside the van. Peter could see his brothers were with him. They were in a hurry. His dad waved goodbye to Father and ran towards the van, yelling at the boys to climb in.

Thomas yelled at Peter to get in his car seat. Peter obeyed because he wanted to get going too. Once the van was moving, Peter looked back at the house. It was soundless; no sight of the Goat Woman. He didn't believe what he saw and he knew no one else would either. He decided the only person he would tell would be his mom. The house shrank in the window as they drove away until it was invisible.

With the house out of his view, Peter calmed down and realized he was soaked from urine and sweat, and he was freezing. No one noticed he was trembling, which made him miss his mom because she would have noticed. He tried to clench his teeth to stop his jaw from quivering, he fought tears to no avail. Hot tears welled in his eyes and melted the iciness on his cheek as they fell. His dad raced down the streets toward the hospital, and his brothers were silent. Peter sat in the backseat, sobbing uncontrollably and nobody noticed.

Eight

ANNE

"What are you thinking about?" Anne asked Thomas as she returned to Peter's bedside from her shower in the hospital bathroom. She had dressed in the clothes Shiloh had packed for her, black yoga paints and an oversized hooded sweatshirt that said, "World's Okayist Mom". It had been a present from Tane a few years back. Her normally perky blond curls were wrapped into a bun on top of her head. She felt like a wet noodle as she sat in the corner chair across from Peter's hospital bed. She slouched way down into the chair and pulled up a blanket.

"I was thinking about what you said about when Shiloh was born. It seems so long ago when he was little and the other kids were all at home too. Time goes by so fast. One minute they want you to hold them, and you can't put them down for a second or they get mad. Then, the next minute, they don't return your phone calls."

"Yeah, I remember when Shiloh was little. That was a rough time for me," Anne shared her memory of his first day home from the hospital. "I remember trying to adjust to a baby with Peter's school issues going on. It was really hard."

. . .

Anne reminisced about the first day she and her beautiful, new baby, Shiloh, were back at home. Anne was trying to get back into the swing of managing the household, plus nursing a new baby while healing up from child birth. Thomas had agreed to drive the kids to school for a few weeks, so Anne didn't have to take Shiloh out in the cold, December air.

To say Anne was overwhelmed was an understatement. It was as if all the closets and dressers decided to vomit out their contents at the same time, leaving laundry littered in every possible space imaginable. When she arrived home, her heart sank as her feet crunched the overlooked glass that was still on the walkway outside the window that Paul and Tane had broken. The boys had not been punished yet, and Anne still had to talk to Peter about his school stuff. They also had the Christmas concert at the school early next week. Plus, Anne was planning Shiloh's baptism with the whole extended family for the following weekend. Anne's head was spinning; *I wish I could have a maid.*

Anne and Shiloh were enjoying a few quiet hours before the kids got back from school. Anne watched Shiloh as he dozed off to sleep. *He's so beautiful. He looks so much like Paul and Tane. What a gift he is to our family.* Anne laid him in the crib, turned the monitor on, and decided to tackle the laundry. As she headed down the hall to the bathroom, she heard the phone ringing. *Don't wake up Shiloh!* She hustled to the phone. Caller ID showed it was the school; Anne's heart plummeted.

"Hello," Anne spoke softly, trying not to wake Shiloh.

"Anne, it's Val. How are you?"

"Hi Val. I'm alright."

"How's that baby? Ready to make an entrance?"

"Oh, he's here. He came on Friday," Anne sounded exhausted.

"Oh my, I didn't know. I'm sorry to bug you then; I had no idea. He must have been a little early?"

"Yeah, a few weeks. We're okay, though. What can I help you with, Val?" Anne was scared to ask, and she felt like she already knew the answer.

"I can call Thomas."

"No, just tell me, and I can get a hold of Thomas if I need to."

"Well, Peter's having a rough day."

"What's going on?"

"He's been crying all morning. Mrs. Krieg had him in her office for a while, but she had to leave town. He was upset when he got here this morning. It escalated when he didn't have a bag lunch and tuna was on the menu. He was having raging fits in the classroom. He threw things out of his desk and then he knocked his classmate's desk over onto the ground – with her still sitting there."

"It's tuna day again? How often do you serve that?" Anne immediately felt guilty. *I didn't know it was tuna day. I didn't check the lunch menu because I was in the hospital.*

"What do you want us to do? He can't be disrupting class. Do you want to come get him or what?" Val continued.

Anne rubbed her forehead temples. *I just need a break from this school drama for one day.* "I'll call Thomas to come get him."

She hung up the phone and dialed Thomas's cell phone. "Thomas, the school called. Peter needs to be picked up."

"What happened?"

"He's upset, disrupting the class because he didn't get a bag lunch, and it's tuna day. Can you go get him?" Anne checked the baby monitor. Shiloh was perfect, complete with a little baby smile.

"Yep. Anything else you need?"

"No." Anne hung up the phone again and mournfully went to fold her piles of laundry.

* * *

Anne giggled at the memory of it. "I'll never forget those piles of laundry. Every color, size, and shape was represented like a melting pot. I seriously think if there were a world record for that sort of thing. I should've entered the contest."

Thomas laughed. He remembered getting Peter from school that day. "Those years were tough, but I would go back to them in a New-York minute. Do you remember where I found Peter when I got to the school?"

"I don't know if I do? Those years are just a haze to me. Was he with Val?" Anne asked.

Thomas laughed again with a smile on his face as he retold his experience that day.

* * *

THOMAS

After Thomas had arrived at school, there was no sign of Peter. Val came out of her office and said, "He went into Mrs. Polly's room." She pointed to a room across the hall.

Thomas shrugged his shoulders in confusion. "I thought he had music at 11:00?"

"We don't have the staff to deal with this stuff anymore. He couldn't stay in his classroom. Mrs. Krieg's gone, and I've been trying to help sub the gym class today. He wanted to go in there and Mrs. Polly didn't mind. I didn't have anywhere else to put him," Val said in a defensive tone.

Thomas walked across the hall and was going to enter the room when he heard music and kids singing. He looked through the window on the door and he saw older kids. Tane was sitting on a chair in the back row. Tane saw his dad, and he waived. Thomas waved back, and then he saw Peter sitting on the piano bench next to the teacher. Thomas waited for the end of class, which took about fifteen minutes. The kids walked out of the door in single file. Tane was one of the last students out the door; he saw his dad and called out, "Dad, are you here to get Peter?"

"Yeah. Why's he in there?"

"He just likes it in there. He's really good at playing the piano."

"Okay. . . Bud, I'll see you after school when I pick you up," Thomas waved to Tane, who walked in line with his class, which was leaving. Thomas walked into the now, nearly- vacant room. Peter was still sitting at the piano, but he looked happy. Mrs. Polly walked around placing music sheets on the chairs to get ready for the next class. Looking up, she noticed Thomas, but it took her a minute before she recognized him as Peter's dad.

"Mr. Arnold."

"Dad," Peter called as he jumped down from the piano and ran over to him.

"Hi, how are you guys?" Thomas asked Peter, but he looked to Mrs. Polly for an answer.

"We're great. Peter's the best helper." Mrs. Polly winked at Thomas. She had a smile on her face that matched the cheery colors of her sweater. "I forgot something in the copy machine. I'll be right back." She stuck a pencil behind her ear, which was barely visible in her red mop of hair, and she left the room.

"Peter, why are you not in your classroom?" Thomas asked.

"Dad, I can't be there. They had tuna again! I didn't have a lunch. My teacher told me I had to eat the tuna, but I couldn't. The kids were all making fun of me, but I was good. I waited until the lunch bell rang, so they had to let me go back to class. But once I got back to my desk, I could smell the tuna on Aiden, who sits next to me; it was so *bad*. The teacher wouldn't let me move, so I had to do something to get out."

Thomas didn't have the patience for Peter's whining. "So, you got in trouble on purpose so you could get out of the class. How did you end up in music class?"

"I just came in here because Val said she didn't want me in her office. I didn't have anywhere to go. Mrs. Polly's my friend."

"Son, that is not appropriate. We need to go, so Mrs. Polly can work. You can't be bothering other teachers. You need to learn to stay in *your* classroom." Thomas grabbed Peter by the hand, leading him out the door. He waived at Mrs. Polly, who was down the hall and called, "Thank you!"

"No problem," Mrs. Polly said.

Thomas was in a hurry to get out of the building. *It's so embarrassing always having to come here and take care of these little episodes with Peter. Things have to get better soon.* Val met them by the front door as they were trying to make an escape.

"I grabbed his homework from his teacher." She handed Thomas a stack of books and a folder. "Mrs. Krieg isn't here right now, but she's going to want to talk to you again. She needs you to follow through with the behavior evaluation," Val pressed.

"Thanks for the help, but I gotta go." Thomas pushed through the door, holding Peter's hand, without looking back.

Nine

PETER

A nurse wearing bright, purple cloud scrubs walked into Peter's room to adjust his IV solution and take his vitals. In a lighter sleep, Peter was aware of her presence and the cold fluid she pushed through the IV into his vein. He was alone in the room as his parents left to order dinner. He tried to open his eyes to see the nurse, but couldn't; he was just so tired. He had vaguely heard his parents talk about the trouble he had experienced in school. Those were hard memories for him to relive. Drifting deeper now and letting sleep win, his dreams led him into a replay of a childhood memory he would never forget.

• • •

The night of his kindergarten, Christmas concert quickly arrived. Ecstatic for his performance, Peter wanted to wear his Sunday clothes to sing his solo. Thomas dropped Peter off at the school thirty-minutes early for voice warm ups and line up with his class. Meanwhile, Anne wrestled with the clock back home to get four kids out the door on time. She made it, barely.

It was time to start the concert and all the kids had to line up, so when they walked onto stage, they were arranged by height. Peter could feel his nerves tighten in his stomach and bladder. He quickly raised his hand, but blurted out his question before his classroom teacher, Mrs. Larth, could called on him, "Can I go to the bathroom?"

"No, Peter. You just had a break before we started the lineup. It's time to start the show. Look, Mrs. Polly's already taking the first group of kids to the gym." She pointed to the kids leaving the room.

"No, I have to go." Peter wiggled his lower body.

"You'll have to wait." Mrs. Larth had no sympathy for Peter.

Mrs. Polly motioned for Peter's group of kids to come on stage. It was the last group and they were to stand in the front row. *I could ask Mrs. Polly, but she's over there. I guess I can hold it for a while.* Peter walked in line onto the stage and located his family. They were sitting in the back because they had the baby. Once he was on stage looking out at everyone, he was so excited he forgot he needed to use the restroom.

Mrs. Polly came up to the microphone and introduced herself before announcing the first couple of songs. All the kids sang loudly. *I love singing!* Peter thought. The time went fast, and then it was time for Peter's solo.

Mrs. Polly came to the microphone first and said, "Tonight we have a special treat. We are going to hear one of my favorite Christmas carols, "Away in the Manger", performed by our feature soloist tonight, Peter Arnold, son of Thomas and Anne Arnold. Please help me welcome Peter." She began to clap, waiting for Peter to come to the microphone. Peter's stomach was in a knot. *I'm ready.* Looking at his mom, her eyes were glued to his, and neither one of them broke eye contact. Peter walked to the microphone, waiting for the piano to begin. The room was silent for what seemed like an eternity. His palms were sweating. *Even my brothers are watching me. I'm going to be great!*

Mrs. Polly played the introduction on the piano, and then nodded her head when it was Peter's cue to come in. Peter opened his mouth and perfectly on cue and in pitch, he sang his solo. With each word, his nervousness went away a little more; his muscle's loosened; he could feel that it sounded right. His mom was glowing. Peter never felt more special. *I love this! My mom's so happy with me.* When his short solo ended, something happened he never expected. Everyone got off their chairs, stood up, and clapped loudly. He even heard his brothers call out, "Way to go Peter!"

Peter was speechless. He looked to Mrs. Polly. She stood facing him; she held one arm across her waist and the other behind her to fake a bow, trying to get Peter to take one. Giggling, he imitated her, and bowed all the way down. Some parents laughed because it was so cute, but most clapped harder. *They liked it! They liked me!*

Peter felt like he found his place. He wanted to stand forever in this magical moment. *People are never this nice to me. Even my mean, old teacher, Mrs. Larth, is smiling and clapping.* He must have stood at the microphone a few minutes too long because Mrs. Polly started to nod for him to return. Peter sighed with relief and turned to go back to his spot. He didn't even know he had been holding in all that air. It was like the last little bit of nerves were getting released as he walked back to his spot, and then something terrible started happening.

It's happening . . . and I can't stop it! He looked to the door to see if he could run, but it was too far. *Oh God, please don't let me do this now!* The more he tried holding it, the harder it came. *I'm peeing my pants! Oh no!* Tears filled his eyes, but didn't dare fall. His whole body shook. He reached his spot, but stayed facing the wall. *I can't turn around!*

Mrs. Polly walked right up to the stage and whispered, "Peter, turn around."

Peter stood with his feet glued to the stage, viciously shaking his head back and forth. Mrs. Polly could hear him quietly crying, "No, no, no, no."

"Peter, turn around," she called again. Now every last set of eyes in the room was directly focused on Peter. *I gotta get off this stage! The door's all the way on the other side of the room, and I have to face everyone to go that way. There's no other way! Why now?* He slowly started to turn to see his exit, and then once he saw it, he darted off the side of the stage as best he could – for a kid wearing leg braces.

With a view only a few feet away, Mrs. Polly saw Peter run off the stage. She was also the first to see his tear-streaked cheeks, his red ears, and the stain down his pants. Her heart sank; she just let him go.

Anne saw the whole thing as well. When she saw Peter start to run off the stage, she could see the tears, and she could also see why. With her stomach in her throat, she got up out of her chair and started to weave through the audience to meet Peter at the door. Whispers buzzed all over the room. Lots of the younger kids were laughing. With tunnel vision, Anne ran to her baby. "Shut up you idiots! He has an undeveloped urinary system," Anne muttered as she squeezed past a group of three boys laughing hysterically. She elbowed one of the boys in the back of the head. "It may or may not have been an accident that your fat head was in my way," Anne whispered.

Peter ran straight ahead even though he could barely see through his tears. He could see someone blocking the doorway. As he got closer, he saw his mom, his sweet mom, who just a moment ago beamed with so much pride. He flew into her arms, and she scooped him up. Peter begged her through his sobs, "Mama, make me invisible! Please!"

Anne reached into her purse with a trembling hand to pull out her aviator sunglasses and placed them on Peter. She held him to her chest. She blinked back tears, cleared her throat, and in a squeaky, mouse whisper, she sang directly into his ear.

"Make me invisible, I don't want to see this man behind me staring at me. Lord can you help me, help me be brave. Lord I need you. I need to be saved."

As Anne sang, she walked out the back of the gym. Mrs. Polly restarted the concert and a cheery "Grandma Got Ran over by a Reindeer" rang out. As Anne walked down the hall towards the front exit, Peter's cries softened to whimpers. His face felt hot. *I want to die,* he thought.

Anne carried Peter to the van, humming her song softly on his cheek. Neither Anne nor Peter said anything in the van. Peter sat in back being invisible with the sunglasses on while the radio played an instrumental version of "Mary Did You Know". Looking through the window, they watched as the first tiny, white snowflakes of the season fell poetically onto the ground. *I don't ever want to go to this school again. I hate it. It makes my tummy hurt.*

After about ten minutes of watching the snow, the rest of the family piled into the van. Thomas opened the side door to lock Shiloh's car seat in place. He saw Peter sitting in back with Anne's sunglasses on; he knew the game he was playing. "Where's Peter?" he asked Anne.

"He left after the concert. He's probably at home right now." Anne winked at Thomas.

"Well, we'd better get back. I'm going to have taco pizza delivered to the house. I don't want him to eat it all," Thomas said with a grin. *I'm not hungry. Don't talk to me,* Peter thought. *Today was the best moment of my life and the worst.*

Ten

ANNE

After soiling himself at his concert in the most horrid night of his life, Peter had disappeared into his room. When the pizza arrived and the rest of the family dug in, Anne asked Thomas to set two pieces aside for Peter because she was busy nursing Shiloh. Thomas quickly complied with her request, grabbing a third piece for Anne. *Life with five kids means I always have to be multitasking, and I pretty much never get warm food,* Anne sighed as she longingly smelled the out-of-reach pizza.

When Anne was able to make it into the kitchen, she picked up the piles of greasy napkins that the family had left at the table and threw the empty pizza boxes in the overstuffed trash. Anne had previously picked up a movie, *The Lion King,* to watch now as part of the concert post-party celebration, but nobody was celebrating. Thomas offered to take Shiloh back to their room to put him down for bed. Anne managed to get all the kids, except Peter, into the family room. She passed out blankets and pillows to commence movie night. Once the kids were all engrossed in the movie, she snuck out; she had to see Peter. She grabbed his pizza and extra taco-sauce packets. As she walked, she pulled off the bigger chunks of lettuce from his pizza as those always made Peter gag. She hid the diced tomatoes under the Doritos, which he loved. *Anything to get this kid to eat a vegetable.*

His door was closed, but not all the way; she could see a sliver of light coming from the narrow crack. Anne approached it, pressing her face up against the opening. Peter had changed into his green Ninja-Turtle pajamas, but he still had her sunglasses of invisibility on. He was looking at some picture books. Anne gently knocked on the door and stuck her head in pretending to be looking for Peter, "Peter, are you in here? Peter, the light is on, but I can't see you. Hmm, that's funny, I thought he would be in here. . ."

Peter laughed, grabbed his sunglasses, and took them off, "Here I am, Mom." Anne's heart lifted. One thing about Peter, he never stayed mad, or sad, or any emotion, for very long.

"I have taco pizza." Anne slipped through the doorway, carrying the plate in front of her.

Peter's eyes popped wide open as he reached for it. "Taco pizza, yum." Anne sat on the bed with her arm around her son as he ate his pizza. He chewed quickly, with purpose. After his last bite, he set his plate on his nightstand, crawled up onto Anne's lap, and placed his head under her chin. Anne grabbed his hand and began kneading his finger joints to help them relax. In a small voice, Peter asked. "Mama, what's wrong with me?"

Anne inhaled deeply. "Honey, nothing's wrong with you. You are the way God made you. Perfect for you."

"No, Mama. None of the other kids pee their pants all the time."

"Well. . . Peter, you. . .you were born a little too early."

"Like Shiloh?"

"Well no, not like Shiloh. Shiloh was a little early, but he was ready to come out. You weren't ready to come out. You were what is called premature. You were such a miracle baby; so little, and your body didn't have enough time to grow. You had to do a lot of catching up after you were born. You know how you have to wear your braces to help you walk?"

"Yeah," Peter nodded. "No one else has those either."

"Well, no one you know, but some kids in other places wear them too. They straighten and hold up your legs because they can't be strong on their own. Your bladder is also like that. It's a little behind because it didn't get enough time to grow before you were born. Even though you can't see it, it's a muscle like the ones in your legs. It just needs a little more help than most people's." Anne grabbed a bottle of emu oil on Peter's nightstand and dabbed out a dime-size amount into her right palm. She dipped her finger into it and rubbed it into Peter's joints. Peter sighed at the contact of the slow burn the oil created as it cooled his flesh, relieving some of the tightness.

"I don't understand why I have to stick out. I just want to be like everyone else."

"Honey, it's okay to be different. Hey, you know what? You reminded me of something. Do you know at Steep & Brew where they have that fish tank?"

"Yeah."

"Do you know how it's full of plain rocks on the bottom, but there's that plastic ruby sitting on top?

"Yeah."

"That sticks out, doesn't it?" Anne squeezed some more oil out into her palm to use on Peter's other hand. She replaced the bottle on the nightstand.

"Yeah, I always see it."

"Well, it sticks out because it's different than the other rocks. But, since it sticks out, you can see how beautiful it is compared to all the other rocks. If it were in a tank of rubies, nobody would notice it. I think you're like that ruby in the water. You stick out because you're different, but your differences only make you shine brighter."

"Um."

"Peter, it's not your fault, what happened tonight."

"I know, I asked to go to the bathroom, but my teacher wouldn't let me." Peter let out a groan in frustration.

"What? When?"

"Before we got on stage, my tummy got nervous again. I asked to go, but she said, 'No'."

"Who said 'No'?"

"Mrs. Larth. I don't know why she doesn't change her name to Mrs. Barf. I really don't like her."

The pressure in Anne's head began to build, and she could feel her ears getting warm. *This school has got to be the least sympathetic place as they won't even let a five-year-old with a kidney condition go to the bathroom! Then, it leads to the most embarrassing incident in his life!* Anne's mind raced. "Peter, I'll call the school first thing Monday."

Anne sat planning what she was going to tell Mrs. Krieg while Peter leaned onto his mom's shoulder and fell asleep. Anne wasn't surprised as Peter always fell asleep best when he was lying on someone. It was a very high-need quality for him to have, but it was so sweet too. Anne listened for his breath to get heavy, rolled him off of her, and tucked him into bed. She swept his hair out of his face, kissed his cheek, and stole one more look as she left the room. He looked like an angel.

Anne peeked into the family room to see if the movie was still playing. The kids were miraculously behaving. Then, she went searching for Thomas and Shiloh, finding them both asleep in her room; Thomas was reclined with Shiloh on his chest. Anne crawled in bed next to them both. Thomas opened one eye. "How's the soloist?"

"Sad. He asked me what's wrong with him and why the other kids don't pee in their pants."

Thomas raised an eyebrow at Anne to continue. "I told him it was because he was born too soon."

"What did he say?"

"Nothing really. He fell asleep. Isn't there something more we can do for him? What about that urologist at Rochester who he saw before? Maybe now, since Peter is older, there is something . . .?"

Thomas let out a heavy sigh, "Anne, he's lucky he has a urinary system. You saw the way he was born. We're so blessed he's even alive."

"What about an acupuncturist? Someone was telling me that they did needles in the top of the head, and it cured a leaky bladder right up."

"Anne, nothing short of a kidney transplant is going to help that kid," Thomas said as he stared blankly into Anne's eyes.

I just won't accept that there is nothing we can do. Anne started to cry. "It's so hard to watch him go through these trials. He's been through so much in his little life.

Thomas used his free arm to pull Anne into his chest. She rested her face next to Shiloh. The smell of Shiloh's coconut baby-powder tickled her nose, creating a moment of serenity that stopped her tears as Anne dreamed of a beach somewhere. After a few minutes, Anne gained her composure. "I'd better make the rest of the kids go to bed. I want to finish planning the baptism tonight yet, too." Anne got up to finished her night duties.

Eleven

THOMAS

"Pizza's here!" Shiloh called, as he carried a stack of three pizza boxes into Peter's hospital room. Tane followed him. Paul hurried into the room a few seconds behind Tane, with Macey and Johnny in tow. Thomas took the pizza boxes and set them on the rolling food tray in the room. He dished up paper plates and passed them out.

Anne reached out and grabbed Macey, pulling the pigtailed girl onto her own lap. "I miss you. Are you both behaving at Auntie's?" She asked as ruffled Johnny's hair. Johnny's was the kid in the family who didn't match any other member including his twin. His hair was white, his eyes were green, and his personality was that of a little mathematician, even at six-years-old.

Johnny squirmed, "Yes, you know what mom?"

"What?"

"I'm the chubby bunny champ. I got 47 marshmallows in my mouth." He flexed his bicep muscles to prove he was a champion.

Macey budded in, "Yeah, but then the marshmallows exploded all over. Does that count?" She turned to her dad.

Thomas laughed, "Yeah it counts. That's how you celebrate getting all those marshmallows stuffed in your mouth." He looked at Johnny. "You wait until I can challenge you. I'm the ultimate champion."

By now, both twins had noticed their older brother lying in bed. "Is he sleeping?" Johnny whispered.

"Sort of," Thomas said. "Does it scare you?"

"No, he looks like he is sleeping," Johnny said as he shrugged his shoulders.

"Well, then you can think of it like that," Thomas replied.

Macey pulled something out of a red backpack no one had noticed she had even been holding, "I made something for him." She held up an orange paper plate with a hole cut out of the center. "It's a wreath. It's orange because it's his favorite color. Auntie helped me write, 'I love you, Peter'."

Thomas took the wreath from Macey and hung it from the knob on the IV poll next to Peter's bed. "It's beautiful. He'll love it." Thomas could not look at any wreath, even a paper plate one, without being reminded of a very special day a long time ago – Shiloh's baptism.

* * *

It was well over a decade ago when Shiloh's baptism Sunday was celebrated. After the ceremony was over, the kids, except for Peter, played in the church yard waiting for the adults to get done visiting. Peter was too timid to go outside, with the Goat Woman's house looming over the playground. Outside the church, tables were set up with Christmas wreaths for sale. Thomas walked up to Father Raymond to inquire about the wreaths.

"Where did you get all the wreaths?"

"Sister Sarah makes them. We cut the branches from the pine trees out back. She needs money to support her mission here, and this is a new project we came up with."

"So when you were out running around the hills the other night, when you saw my boys, you were out doing this stuff?"

"Sort of. I wear many hats." Father laughed nervously.

"Is this a new mission or is it still to help fund the medical mission I used to volunteer for?" Thomas asked.

"A little of both," Father said.

"Hum, well we'd better buy one since these wreaths helped bring my boys home." Thomas pulled out his wallet. "Maybe I can just get all my Christmas shopping done." He pulled out two crisp bills from his wallet. "Kids, come over here and pick out some wreaths," Thomas called to the kids outside; they listened out of pure curiosity, and then they came in. Thomas looked around for Peter and found him in the front of the church, sitting down at the piano staring at the keys.

"Peter," Thomas called over to him, "Would you like to pick one out, too?" Peter smiled, got up, and limped over to the table. "Is your leg brace bothering you?" Thomas asked with his eyebrows furrowed.

"Yeah, it feels a little tight."

"Here, let me look at it. Yep, I think you must have grown again." Thomas adjusted the width for the metal cross strap. "Try that."

Peter stood up straighter. "That's better. Thanks dad."

"No, problem. Which wreath do you want? We will keep two for our doors at home and we can give the other ones to Grandma Arnold and Grandma Jean." Peter picked one with holly berries and a giant, red bow. By now Anne, with Shiloh in his car seat, had joined them by the table, and they were bundled up in their coats, ready to go.

"Alright family, I have pot stickers in the crockpot at home. Are you all ready?" Anne asked.

"Can I sing my solo?" Peter asked from behind the table. He was smiling and Thomas thought, *why not have a redo with just the family here to listen? It might be nice to have a positive ending.*

"Sure," Thomas said. Anne led Peter's siblings to sit up front by the piano. Peter sat on the bench and flexed his fingers. He struck a chord, and effortlessly played and sung his solo. He finished with the biggest smile on his face.

"It was good, wasn't it?" he asked. Everyone clapped as they wanted him to feel special. Peter stepped down from the piano bench and took a huge bow.

Anne raised her eyebrows, "How do you know how to play it on the piano? Did Mrs. Polly teach you that?"

Peter shook his head, "No, I just picked out the keys. You can hear the sounds if you listen."

"Yeah, but you still have to practice. People don't just play the piano," Thomas questioned as he looked at his son.

"I guess I do," Peter answered boldly with confidence.

Anne and Thomas exchanged glances. "I think he picked that up from Mrs. Polly," Thomas whispered to Anne, who nodded. They shrugged their shoulders, gathered the kids, and the four huge Christmas wreaths Thomas just shelled out $200 to buy, and they headed to the van.

Once inside the van, Peter was fidgety while waiting for Thomas to secure Shiloh in his car seat. "Peter, can you please sit down."

"Dad, I don't want to sit in this seat. I don't like this window. I can see her." Peter's face twisted into a pre-crying tantrum. Thomas turned to look. The house on the hill invited his gaze. The house door was ajar, and a woman was standing on the bottom porch step. Dressed in a grey robe, she was holding two wooden boxes. She was calling out to someone. Thomas looked down the hill and saw Father Raymond walking towards her, carrying a shovel. The woman and Father talked briefly on the porch, and then went inside the house.

Thomas blew it off as he turned back to Peter, who he saw exhale when the house door was closed. "Just sit still. She's gone now,"

Thomas said to ease Peter's anxiety. Peter put his head down and sucked in his lip to prevent it from quivering while he waited for his dad to drive away.

Twelve

ANNE

After dinner at the hospital, Anne was left alone at Peter's bedside. Anne flipped through the TV channels, but the only thing that remotely peaked her interest was a rerun of *The Golden Girls*. After watching it for a moment, she realized her favorite character, Sophia, wasn't in this one, so she shut it off. The room was dark now except for the nightlight above the bed. Anne curled her legs under her as best she could in the small chair. She leaned all the way over against the wall, resting her head on a pillow she had made from her sweatshirt. Closing her tired eyes, Anne drifted to sleep.

A beeping noise sounded. Anne's eyes darted to Peter's monitor. She was just about to jump up and press the nurses call light when she recognized the beep as her cell phone. It was a text from Mrs. Polly. Anne had stayed friends with her after all the years Mrs. Polly taught her kids. She wanted an update, and Anne was disappointed she couldn't give her better news. Mrs. Polly's reply text surprised Anne, it read,

"Exa's beside herself. Have you talked to her?"

Anne didn't know what to say because so much had happened lately with Exa. Surprised why Mrs. Polly would know to ask, it took Anne a while to remember Mrs. Polly was the reason she even met Exa all those years ago.

• • •

It had been the Monday morning after the disastrous Christmas concert, and it was a short school week because of the upcoming holiday. Insanity defined her morning trying to get four kids ready for school, plus nurse a baby. Peter was nowhere to be found at the breakfast table. Anne laid out the cereal boxes and a plate of toast for the kids, and with the baby in a sling, she ran down the hall. "Peter, breakfast!" No answer. She popped her head into his room to see him still in his pajamas. The clothes they had laid out together the night before, to be worn today, were jumbled up on top of the dresser.

"Mama, look at my hands." He held up both hands, each one was knotted into a fist except for his thumbs.

Anne held her hand out to usher him over. "Come here. It'll be faster to just run them under warm water." Peter walked with her to the bathroom and held his fists under the water facet as it streamed water, almost too hot to touch. Anne leaned over the facet as best she could with Shiloh in his baby sling. Being careful not to get Shiloh wet, Anne massaged Peter's fingers one by one, starting at the tip and twisting her fingers along the length of each one until she got to the knuckle. She paid extra attention to the inside of each joint, rubbing it with her thumb until she felt a release. After she was done, she wrapped his fingers in a white, hand towel to dry.

"Alright, now go get dressed." Anne saw in his face the look of determination she knew all too well. His lips where perched out in a way that resembled a beak, and he folded his arms across his chest. Shiloh simultaneously fussed, and she could smell why. In the background, she heard a fight breaking out at the breakfast table.

"Everyone's going to laugh at me," Peter said as he looked to Anne with huge, sad eyes.

"It was a long weekend. I'm sure everyone has forgotten already."

Anne swayed her hips back and forth trying to sooth Shiloh. Shiloh's fussing escalated into a scream, and she knew it was pointless to try to hold a conversation. Peter looked devastated. Anne tried to bounce Shiloh in the carrier, but he screamed louder.

"I want to stay home with you and Shiloh, mom," Peter hollered over the screaming.

Anne sighed, and tried adjusting Shiloh. "One more day. You can stay home *one* more day. I have to change Shiloh before we can load him up in the car seat. Will you get dressed and grab whatever breakfast you can find? I can tell the school that you're not feeling well."

It's not a total lie because he isn't feeling well, even though it's emotional and not physical. I don't know what else to do. There's a war going on in my kitchen, and I can smell a war going on in Shiloh's diaper. The roads are icy, so travel will be slow. I don't have time to fight to get Peter to school only to have to go get him in an hour after he gets kicked out of class. Again.

Peter's face lit up. "Yes, mom," he said as he got up to dress. Anne raced across the hall to change Shiloh, and then hurried into the kitchen. Tiny colored marshmallows and cereal loops were scattered over the floor. Tane and Paul were not in the room. Marie was trying to sweep the cereal off the floor.

"Where are your brothers?"

"They went to the car already. Mom, school started five minutes ago," Marie adjusted her glasses on her nose as she informed Anne. Anne looked to the clock to confirm what she already knew.

"Okay, can you get in the car? Here are my keys. Start it up so it will get warm. I'll be out in two minutes. I have to find my shoes. Peter, get your coat on!"

"Mom, I never ate breakfast," Peter whined.

"We'll have to grab something on the way back from school." Anne made up a solution without even really thinking about what was coming out of her mouth.

"Steep & Brew?" Peter asked.

"Sure."

"What? Peter's not going to school? Why?" Marie asked.

"Marie, listen. Get in the car. Don't talk about it. Peter's not feeling well," Anne fumbled for words.

"Are you kidding? He looks fine to me. I don't want to go to school. Can I go to Steep & Brew?"

Anne grabbed the broom from Marie and whispered in a disciplinary tone just inches in front of Marie's face. "Marie, you're my big girl. You have to listen to me, please. Don't tell your brothers. Just get your stuff on and get in the car." Marie sucked in her lip, grabbed the keys, her coat, and book bag, and went outside. Anne threw the broom against the wall and ran around, getting the last of the stuff for Shiloh and Peter. *I still have my night gown on,* she thought as she looked down. She pulled on her boots anyway, *if I put my coat over the top, no one will notice,* she convinced herself.

Anne dropped the kids off at school and headed home. "Mom, Steep & Brew!" Peter urgently reminded Anne when she didn't turn at the stop because she was headed home.

Anne remembered, but she couldn't believe she agreed to go there. She just said that to get Peter in the car. "Peter, I'm in my pajamas. I can't go to Steep & Brew right now. Can we go for lunch?"

"Mom! Buuuut, I wannnt to, and you said Steep & Brew. You said on the way home!" Peter voice was coming out in high-pitched shrieks. Shiloh fussed as he picked up on the tone of conversation.

Anne looked in the mirror and fluffed her hair. *I don't even have an ounce of makeup on right now.* "I did say that. Alright, we'll go in and order drinks and a muffin, but we'll take our stuff to go."

"Okay," Peter grinned.

By the time they arrived, Shiloh had fallen asleep, tucked in with his elephant print, fleece blanket. Peter announced he had to go to the bathroom and made his way there. Anne ordered drinks and two pumpkin muffins. While she waited, a familiar face popped in the door.

"Mrs. Polly!" Peter called as he ran his stiff "legs-with-braces" run out of the bathroom. "How come you're not at school?"

"I should ask you the same question," Mrs. Polly said as she waved towards Anne, who had turned her head to join in the conversation.

"I'm not feeling well today," Peter announced with a smile. Mrs. Polly laughed and looked back at Anne.

"We had a rough morning and he was nervous, so I told him he could stay home one more day. He's still scared to face the kids," Anne whispered as she covered her mouth pretending to bite her nail. They called Anne's order for pick up and she motioned for Peter to get it. While he was gone, the two ladies talked openly about the accident.

"I'm so sorry about that," Mrs. Polly apologized. "My heart broke. Is he okay?"

"No, we've been busy so we don't have too much time to talk about it, but he's been upset. He has had nightmares, and it was a long weekend." Anne's eyes flashed layers of deep exhaustion. "I just don't know what to do. I mean, emotionally, he's crushed, but, physically, something must be done. He can't go through life like this. I asked Thomas about getting another evaluation with an urologist, but he said nothing could be done except a kidney transplant. That's more of a last resort, so we're stuck in this incredibly embarrassing stage hoping as he grows, he'll get stronger."

"He did such a great job. I was really hoping this would be good for his self-esteem," Mrs. Polly added.

"Hey, can I ask you something while Peter is over there?" Anne leaned in close. Mrs. Polly nodded. "Peter wanted to sing his solo again yesterday for us at church, and well, he went to the piano and he played it on the keys. Did you teach him that?"

Mrs. Polly's face lite up as she waved her hand in excitement, "No, I tried to tell you this when I asked you who taught him piano. He keeps saying he taught himself, but he plays perfectly. He's in my room several times a week; he hears a song, and then plays it. He doesn't read the sheet music. The kid plays by ear."

Anne scratched her head. "Are you sure?"

"Yeah, he's a talent. I know other people who play by ear, but usually they've had some level of training. When I was in college, one of my roommates could play by ear like that; it was amazing. It's sort of weird, though, to think about that now because I'm meeting her here for coffee."

Anne saw Peter was heading back with their order. "So, why are you not at school?" Anne asked Mrs. Polly to change the subject. "Not feeling well?"

"Actually, I'm taking a personal day. Well, a half day as I'm taking first and second period off. I usually have my second and third graders this morning, but their teachers wanted to get them together to go to the dinosaur exhibit down at the museum this morning, so I have some free time."

"What? A field trip? I didn't know about that. That would be Paul and Tane's classes, but they never said." *Oh shoot, I didn't even talk to either of them this morning though because they'd gone out to the car, and Shiloh screamed most of the way to the school.*

"Yeah, they had buses taking them over there for a tour this morning," Mrs. Polly added.

"Thomas had the boys, I mean Thomas was driving the boys last week because I was just home from the hospital. Maybe he knew about it?" Anne asked out loud, but more to herself as she worried.

"Oh, here she is!" Mrs. Polly squealed in excitement as she ran to hug a lady who had just walked in. "I grabbed us a table in the corner. I was just chatting with some friends. Here you have to meet one of my students first," Mrs. Polly exclaimed as she grabbed the lady by the arm and ushered her over to Peter and Anne.

"Peter, this is my friend, Exa. Exa, this is Peter, my star student, and his mother, Anne. Peter plays the piano by ear like you. I was just telling his mom how you were another person I knew that could do that," Mrs. Polly was beaming when she talked about Peter to Exa. Exa perked up and looked over to Peter. She met his eyes and he stared back at her. Anne watched Peter's expression as he stared at Exa, and when their eyes met, Peter's eyes twinkled like he recognized something he had lost.

Exa was tall for a woman, maybe five-feet-ten inches. She had long, black hair, parted in the middle. Bright, blue eyes flashed behind long lashes that were outlined in heavy, black eyeliner and mascara. Her nose was slightly bent, but she had a nice smile. She wore a black, maxi dress with flared sleeves. Peter thought it resembled a witch's Halloween costume.

"Hi, Pe ta, and Anne," Exa spoke with an accent. Peter giggled because of the way she said his name.

"Hi," Peter answered shyly as he hid behind his mom's coat.

"Nice to meet you, Exa. I don't mean to be rude, but we have to go get the baby back home before he wakes up, and it's feeding time. You two enjoy your coffee," Anne said as she pushed Peter towards the door. She had remembered she was in her nightgown still and was embarrassed to be meeting new people. They said their good-byes, and Anne got the boys loaded back in the van. She located her cell phone on the passenger seat where she had left it. There were four missed calls, the school twice and Thomas twice. She dialed the school.

"Hi Val, you called? This is Anne Arnold."

"Yeah, we have two boys here in the office who couldn't go on their field trip this morning because they didn't have their slips filled out. Also, Peter never showed up to class today," Val reported in a monotone voice.

"I have Peter. I was going to call – I forgot. He's sick. I didn't know about the field trip. Can I give you verbal permission over the phone?"

"The busses are gone. They can hang out with me until their classes gets back, I guess. You know, I should get paid for all this babysitting I do for your boys," Val joked, but Anne knew she didn't think it was funny.

"I'm sorry, I didn't know. I was recovering from my hospital stay last week," Anne offered, and then got off the phone to call Thomas. The school had called Thomas too, but he didn't have a clue as to what was going on. They talked for a few minutes as Anne drove. When they got home, Anne hung up the phone and grabbed sleeping Shiloh in his car seat. She reached her other hand out to Peter, his face was peaked. "Honey, what's wrong?"

"Mrs. Polly's friend –" Peter said and started to speak again, but then stopped again.

"Yeah."

"I know her," Peter said.

Anne was a little surprised by how intense his gaze was, but she grabbed his hand and pulled him from the van. It was freezing, and she didn't want Shiloh to wake up. "Yeah, we met her. She was nice." Anne said. "Let's get in the house."

Thirteen

ANNE

The night before school started, after Christmas break, Thomas worked late, volunteering at the free clinic. Anne ran around the house, as normal, making sure the laundry was done and book bags were packed. She knew something was up with Peter when she stopped in his room to drop off his laundry basket. His book bag protruded from his garbage can. "Peter, why is your book bag in your garbage when I asked you to get it ready and set it by the door for tomorrow?"

"I'm not going," Peter stated boldly with his arms crossed over his chest with his chin tucked down.

Anne stepped forward towards him. "Honey, I know I let you stay home before, but you have to go back to school tomorrow. You missed three days, and your teacher and friends are probably all worried about you."

"I don't have any friends," Peter said matter-of-factly, crushing Anne's heart.

"What about Mrs. Polly and music class?" She touched his shoulder. Anne could see the wheels turning in Peter's head.

"What if she is gone having coffee again?"

"No, she was only gone one day because her classes were canceled. She'll be there. How about you go back tomorrow so you can see her, and, if it's bad, we can talk about doing something different?"

"Alright mom," Peter agreed without making eye contact. Anne was grateful Peter had a special bond with his music teacher. She gave his shoulder a squeeze and left the room. *Battle won but get ready for the war in the morning . . .*

The next morning went smoothly as all the kids did as they were told. It was like a little heaven to Anne as she drove home from dropping them off. She was going to have six hours alone with Shiloh, and she couldn't have appreciated it more!

Anne and Shiloh cuddled, napped, and picked up left over Christmas decorations. Anne had just laid Shiloh down for his afternoon nap, and was going to grab a shower, when her phone rang. Her heart sank. She didn't even look at the caller ID.

"Val?"

"Mrs. Arnold, how are you?"

"What's wrong?"

"Anne, I really tried not to call you, but things are so out of hand. You need to come get Peter."

"Now? I just put Shiloh down for a nap. I can't wake him. He'll be a total fuss butt," Anne blurted out. "What's wrong with Peter?"

"He won't go to his classroom; he refuses. He said he's only here to see Mrs. Polly, and he has been in her room all morning. Mrs. Polly tolerates it, but we can't run a school like this. Mrs. Krieg tried to physically remove him from the music room, and he freaked. He started kicking and biting her. If he's worried about kid's teasing him, he does it to himself by acting out this way."

Anne was silent as she could visualize Peter doing that, *I did tell him last night to go to school just to see Mrs. Polly. However, I didn't think he would take it literally and just hang out in her room all day. Was this my fault?* "Where's he now?

"He's in the music room. Anne, between you and I, Mrs. Krieg has had it. She's been on the phone all morning talking to the superintendent, trying to figure out what she can do. She wants to talk to you when you come."

"Can you give me an hour? *Please,* Val. I just put Shiloh down, and if he doesn't nap for at least a half hour, my life is going to be unbearable. Please Val, you have kids; you raised kids. Please just stall for me?"

"Okay, one hour," Val agreed.

Anne hung up the phone and checked the monitor. Shiloh was still sleeping. She had time to grab a shower and slip into something other than sweat pants. Something about not having showered in a day makes a person feel vulnerable and weak. She called Thomas to beg him to meet her at the school. He hesitated, but he agreed to let his physician assistant handle his appointments. After exactly thirty minutes, Anne woke up Shiloh to load him in his car seat. *If I don't have trouble with traffic, I should get to the school five-minutes early.*

Pulling into the visitor's parking lot in front of the school, she thought to herself, *this spot should have my name on it already.* Thomas was waiting by the front door. He was in a good mood, as always. She smiled internally as she watched him wave at her. "Hi, sweetie," he called to her. His dark hair ruffled in the wind, indicating that he needed a haircut, but Anne loved it like that. Thomas grabbed Shiloh's car seat from Anne, and took her hand in his free hand. He was her rock.

"I'm nervous," Anne said as the three of them walked into the office to await the meeting.

Val was not in the office, but Mrs. Krieg's door was open. Anne peeked inside. There was no happy-playing-dinosaurs together on the floor with Peter going on today. Mrs. Krieg sat at her desk with her arms crossed and initiated a stare down by refusing to break eye contact with Anne. "Arnolds. Come in here, please."

Thomas and Anne walked inside her office, closing the door behind them. Peter wasn't in the room. Silence deafened the room – except for the buzzing of a fan. "Val informed you about the little circus we have going on today? Peter's camped out in the music room."

"Yeah, I'm sorry. He's just off because he had such a long break. I'll talk to him," Anne offered.

"Mrs. Arnold, your son assaulted me. He's delinquent in more areas than just academics. I talked to the school board and the superintendent. We're going to require Peter to get an evaluation by the school's consulting psychiatrist, Dr. Brown. Peter must be in compliance with any recommendations by Dr. Brown before he will be allowed back in this building," Mrs. Krieg stated without batting an eyelash.

"What? He can't come back?" Anne asked.

"Peter's expelled until he has a behavior plan ready-to-be implemented, with Dr. Brown's help," Mrs. Krieg restated. "Here are his books. His teacher gave a summary of her lessons plans for the next couple weeks, so he doesn't get behind. I called Dr. Brown's office, and he recommended it would take at least a couple weeks to get the full evaluation done as he requires several visits."

"I can't teach him this. I have a new baby," Anne stared blankly at the books.

"Get a tutor then. I can have Val email you a list of tutors in the district who we have worked with before. I've tried everything. My school cannot have this commotion any longer; this is not the place for it. Now, it's your turn to do something. He's not welcome back until Dr. Brown tells me directly he's okay to come back. Take his books. Go get Peter from Mrs. Polly's room. Arnie, the janitor, will escort you all out."

Anne looked to Thomas to say something to change Mrs. Krieg's mind. This was the fastest, most direct meeting they had ever had, and they never got a word in. *This was so wrong!* Thomas reached for the books, wrapped his other arm around Anne, and said, "I agree this is not the place for Peter. We'll get our son; you don't have to make him your problem again. Thank you." Anne's jaw dropped, but then she stood up to follow Thomas.

They walked across the hall to the music room. Through the window, they saw Mrs. Polly directing the class in singing, "*The Farmer in the Dell*". Peter was perched at the piano playing the song for class. He wore the biggest smile Anne had ever seen on him. She pointed her finger and glanced at Thomas. "He's playing the piano." Arnie stepped forward to open the door, but Anne pushed her hand in front and pleaded. "Wait, I have to see this." Anne stepped closer.

Anne and Thomas observed Peter play the piano like it was an old friend. They saw this vibrant smile that was foreign to his face. The usually pale undertones in his face were rosy, and he looked exuberant! Anne whispered, "I never told you because I guess I forgot, but we ran into Mrs. Polly before Christmas break. She said, 'He plays by ear, and it's a rare talent'. I had a hard time believing it, but now I can see it – it's amazing. I can't believe he can even do that with his hands; it's like a miracle. Do you think we should let him? Won't it make it worse?"

"I guess we'll just have to see," Thomas said.

"I don't want to see him get more disappointed if it makes his hands hurt worse."

"I think if this is what he wants to do, then we should encourage it." Then in a voice just above a whisper Thomas said, "Peter's a miracle that no one will ever fully understand. This school is great for kids like Tane and Paul, who make friends easily and play sports. Anne, it's time we face it. Peter's drowning here. He rarely makes it through a whole day, and we spend more energy doing damage control. He's meant for something else," Thomas said, then pushed the door open and went inside to retrieve an all–too-eager-to-go-home, Peter. And just like that, Peter never set foot in a traditional classroom again.

Fourteen

Two weeks into homeschooling, Anne was surprised at how it was working out beautifully; she loved the extra time with Peter. She especially loved not having to visit the principal regularly. Today, Anne dropped Paul and Tane off at their school and Marie off at the middle school. She, Shiloh, and Peter were driving home when all the sudden, KABLAM! A boom under the hood of the van preceded black smoke that filtered into the air like a blanket. Anne's heart beat rapidly as she swerved over to the side of the road, flung her door open, jumped out of the car, viciously yanked Shiloh's door open and grabbed his car seat. "Peter, get out of your seat! The van's on fire. Grab my hand; we're going to run across the street!"

Two boys in hand, Anne scurried to get away from the van. *I don't know if that thing is going to explode or what. I've never seen anything like it.* She reached the sidewalk, two guys in a white, work truck pulled over. One of the men got out with a fire extinguisher and blasted carbon dioxide from it directly at the van's hood. Anne trembled as she watched her van burn – just one minute ago she and her two babies were inside.

Thick, dirty smoke gusted in their direction from the high winds, and Peter couldn't stop coughing long enough to catch his breath. It was well below zero degrees outside, and they were not dressed to stay outside. They needed shelter fast or they would get frostbite.

"Mom, Steep & Brew!" Peter called as he pointed down the block two streets, almost as if he were reading her mind. Anne nodded a big "Yes". She waved to the men in the work truck as they rushed past them. Anne looked back to take notice that the work truck said D & E Electric. She knew she would want to get a hold of them later to thank them properly.

The men waved Anne and the boys away as they understood. Once inside, Anne got out her phone to call Thomas. "Thomas, my van blew up; it was on fire." Anne paced the entryway of Steep & Brew.

"It did? Are you okay?" Thomas asked.

"Yeah, I got the boys out by myself, and some guys in a truck put out the fire. It was scary. My heart's racing," Anne said breathlessly as she put her hand over her heart to feel the thumping in her chest. She leaned against the wall and rested her head all the way back against it to steady herself.

"Where are you now?"

"We ran to Steep & Brew. It's freezing outside."

"Yeah, it's minus fifty with wind chill. Where's the van?"

"On the side of the road. Should I call someone?"

"I can call a tow truck for you." Thomas let out a heavy sigh. "Well, that's really scary; I'm glad you're safe. Anne, I need to get to the hospital before 9:00 a.m. because I have a patient who's headed in for hip surgery with the bone specialist, and I haven't had time to sign off on it yet. I can get down there to pick you up after that, but it'll be about an hour. Is that alright or do you want to call a cab?"

"I think we can wait for you. I see Peter's already pointing to the fish tank. Just call me if it's going to be longer than an hour, and I can, maybe, call my sister."

"Okay, I love you," Thomas said.

"Love you, too," Anne said before she ended the call with shaky hands.

"Mrs. Polly!" Peter exclaimed. Anne turned her head to see she had been wrong about Peter pointing to the fish tank. Mrs. Polly was sitting in a private booth next to it. Anne chuckled as she realized this must be a favorite stop of others as well.

"Mrs. Polly! Hi, do you remember me?" Peter ran up to her table.

Mrs. Polly smiled. It had only been two weeks since Peter attended her class, "Of course, I remember my best music student."

"I miss you. I miss music class. I have to stay home for school now. I like it because I can get done faster, but I don't get to sing or go to your class," Peter rambled. Anne watched his expression as he poured out his heart to her in just a few minutes. Anne had no idea Peter had missed attending her class that much. She continued to be the bystander as Peter talked to Mrs. Polly, witnessing what was obviously to be a very special relationship to Peter. After a few minutes, Anne stepped forward, putting her arm around Peter's shoulders. "Good morning, please don't tell me I forgot about another field trip?" she joked.

"No, field trips today. My classes were canceled because they need my classroom."

"Oh, for what?" Anne asked.

"They use my room to set up the school art show. I don't have music classes because I don't have a classroom. Instead of going to music class, students go with their teachers to the art show. It works out the same since they are both fine art classes. So, I get a few extra days to prep and take some personal time. Since I don't have a classroom to work in, I came here. So yeah, in a long way of answering, you didn't miss a field trip. You should be good."

"Phew, I was worried for a second," Anne said.

"Can I come visit you?" Peter blurted out. Anne was taken aback by the directness of his request since he was normally shy.

"Honey, Mrs. Polly's busy when she's in school. You don't go to her school anymore." Anne tried to explain in a hushed voice as she really had never expected a conversation like this to come up.

"It's okay, Anne," Mrs. Polly said. "Peter, I would love for you to visit me. I miss you too. We're visiting right now though. Isn't that cool?"

"No, it's not. I like being in your class and playing the piano. It's the only thing that makes my tummy not tight," Peter stated softly. Anne soaked up Peter's words, and they stung. It was unfortunate that by leaving school, he had to leave the one thing Anne witnessed to help him with his anxiety.

"Honey, Mrs. Polly has to work when she's at school. I'm sure that if she could have guests in her class she would let you, but there are rules against that sort of thing. Here, can you take my wallet and go order our drinks? How about you pick out a muffin too?" Anne wanted to change the subject fast because she could see little tears starting to glisten as they welled up in the bottom of Peter's eyes. Peter listened, leaving to order drinks.

"I'm sorry, we're still adjusting to the homeschool thing. He really likes you, as you know. He'll just need some time to understand."

"Don't apologize, I adore Peter, and I get it. I get it more than you probably do," Mrs. Polly stated as she looked lovingly to Peter.

"What do you mean more than I do?" Anne squinted her eyes in confusion.

"It's just from one musician to another. I get what his heart feels like when he's with music. It's his passion. He's a kid, but he knows what his heart feels. It's like when you finally find that one thing in your life that makes you, you; it becomes your lifeboat for the rest of the yucky stuff in life. To be away from it is like to be mourning the loss of a soulmate.

"Huh? You lost me. Musician? He was in kindergarten music class." Anne's eyebrow arched.

"Look, you know him as his mother, but I know how his eyes twinkle when he hits the right keys and the sound's perfect. I know — I get the same way. It's a shame to deprive him of something so naturally therapeutic for him. Some people go their whole lives and never find their thing. He's lucky to find it now; think of how it can grow with him?" Mrs. Polly said.

"So, what are you saying? Now, I feel bad for having him at home. I don't have any music skills. Do I get him in piano lessons?" Anne asked.

"You could. Peter's different though. Most piano teachers are like me; people who love music and have trained for years. I don't know if that would do him justice. It might be too rigid."

"What do you mean?"

"Well lessons, you know, are teachers handing over sheet music, requesting you play it over and over until you learn it. Peter plays the piano by ear. He feels it. I think lessons would be draining and uninspiring to an artist like himself."

"Okay, so what then? I can't send him to your class, and you say lessons are too ordinary. What do I do?" Anne said a little defensively.

Mrs. Polly rubbed her face with her hands, thinking hard. "It's like he just needs to be around it and let it absorb into him, so he can learn about it for himself. He'll probably tell you where he wants to go with it. You know. . . I'm may be crazy to think this – let alone bring it up without even knowing what her answer will be – but I really wonder if my friend, Exa, would be able to work with him."

"That lady you were here with last time?" Anne could never forget the name, Exa.

"Yeah, that's her, I forgot I introduced you to her. She just moved back to town and is on a personal sabbatical. Remember, I told you she can play piano by ear; she's never taken a lesson."

"Yeah, you did say that," Anne said.

"She's a world-famous, classical pianist. You would get goose-bumps if you heard her play," Mrs. Polly added.

"I didn't know that, but I don't know anything about classical music either. Is it like Mozart?" Anne shifted on her feet as she leaned over to check on Shiloh asleep in his car seat.

"Some of it is, but there are newer composers now. But in addition to her playing, she has worked as a music therapist, and she might be able to work with Peter. Of course, I'm just thinking of this as I'm saying it. I have no idea what she would say, but why don't you let me ask her?"

"Well you know more about this than I do, but if she's so famous, why would she do therapy?"

"She used to do the therapy when she was still starting her career. She hasn't in a long time, but she isn't working on any projects now, so maybe if I ask for a favor . . . I mean, even if she just sits and hears him play one time, she might be able to give some direction on how to help him nurture his talent."

"Well, it can't hurt to ask, right?"

"No, it can't, and I would love to do this for Peter. I adore your son, and it does bother me to see him upset about losing his access to music class. I'll call her and get back to you. Does that sound like a plan?"

"Sounds good," Anne said. *What could it hurt to check into something?* Peter was balancing the drinks on a tray as he walked towards them. Anne held her hand up in a wave toward Mrs. Polly as she took steps toward Peter, "Thank you for the advice. I see that Peter has our drinks and he's headed toward our usual booth in the back, but I'll wait to hear from you."

"For sure, it was great running into you two, and I'll be in touch." Mrs. Polly flashed a big smile and a wave.

Exactly two weeks later, driving a new, pearl-white mini-van, Anne, Peter, and Shiloh were headed to Exa's house for a "consultation". Anne drove around the block in an unsuccessful search of the house. She decided to take a chance on the only house on the block, which looked like nobody was home. She pulled up next to an old, peach, brick building. It stood tall and sat on the corner lot, looking as though it could have been a commercial building. This house matched the description Exa had given Anne. She had been warned there were no numbers on the house to mark the address as it was actually a century-old-hospital currently under renovation into living quarters.

Everything about the house was ancient. The sidewalk was broken with weeds growing through the cracks. Anne and Peter carefully stepped over the cracks in the cement until they reached the front door and knocked, but they heard no answer. Piano music rolled through the air. Anne pounded on the door and called, "Hello! Exa! Hello!"

The music stopped and they heard measured footsteps getting louder as Exa approached the door and swung it wide open. "Ah hello, Anne and Pe ta, come in!"

Peter loved the way she said his name and he was instantly memorized by her. She was wearing all black again – another maxi dress with black boots. Her blue eyes met each of theirs for a second as she greeted them; her eyes were beautiful, but dull.

"Hi Exa, thank you for agreeing to this visit. We're looking forward to it. Peter, do you remember Ms. . . . ." Anne looked to Exa for a last name.

"Oh, just call me Exa."

"Are you sure?" Anne asked.

"Well yes, my last name I go by is Scarletta and that's even harder for kids to pronounce."

"Scarletta?" That's unique. Is it from around here?" Anne tried to make small talk as she leaned over to help Peter take off his snow boots and coat. Anne could tell Peter was nervous as she pulled his foot out of his boot because his leg muscles were unusually tense. She rubbed his back and whispered, "Relax, this will be fun."

Exa answered Anne's question, "Well no, it's from nowhere. It's a stage name. I don't want people to know my real name."

Peter piped up. "What's a stage name?"

Exa turned to Peter. "It's what people make up when you don't want other people to know your real name. Lots of actors and authors have stage names. For an author, it's called a pen name, but it serves the same purpose. They can have their careers separate from their private lives. I always wanted to be famous, so as soon as I started music school, I changed my name to Exa Scarletta. That's how people know me."

Peter looked confused. "What's an Exa?"

Anne interrupted. "Peter, please don't ask so many questions."

Exa waved her hand to confirm that his question was okay. "Actually, Exa was my great-grandmother's name. She lived in the south on the family plantation that had been in her family for well over a century. They employed a black family. Can I say that? Black family?"

"I don't know, African American, I think is what's now politically correct," Anne said.

"Well anyway, so they had slaves a long time ago, but when slavery ended, my family had African American's working for them who never wanted to leave to get other jobs. Their families were intertwined with mine. They stayed employed with my family for many generations; they became an extension of our family. The women always worked as nannies, and a lot of times, they got to name the babies. That's how my great-grandmother got the name Exa; her nanny named her. I think it might be popular down on the bayou. I always thought it was unique so, I had to steal it. Then, I needed an equally sophisticated last name, and I love *Gone with the Wind*, so I came up with Scarletta."

"That's fascinating," Anne said as she stood back up, and lifted Shiloh's car seat, carrying it through the foyer. "I guess, I thought you were European with your accent."

"Well, my father's folks are Southern. My mother was from here. I got my education in boarding schools overseas – mostly London. I guess it wore off."

"That had to be amazing . . . to grow up in Europe. You were lucky. I have always wanted to travel."

Exa wrinkled her nose. "Lucky, um, no. More, sort of, pushed away. My mom remarried and her husband didn't want me around. They just couldn't really be, um, bothered." Exa squatted down to eye level with Peter. "So, Mr. Pe ta, just remember, if you want to be famous, you need a cool name." She winked at him. Peter didn't hear a word she had spoken because he was staring at the house interior. As soon as they stepped inside through the door that lead from the foyer, they entered a room that used to be the hospital lobby. The original architecture style of the hospital was Victorian and the lobby – which was yet to be remodeled –reflected many ornate features in the wood work and wall coverings.

A huge, open room with cathedral ceilings loomed before them. Natural light poured in through the large, rectangular windows. Wood floors met ash-colored, brick walls. On the furthest wall was a gray, stone fireplace that glowed dark yellow and orange in the center, from a log that was barely visible. Even with the fire, the room was cold. In the middle of the room was something Peter thought was magnificent – a huge mahogany-wood, grand piano! It was not a baby one, but a full-size, grand piano. Peter had never seen a piano that big. White candles were scattered all over the top of the piano, but none of them were currently lit.

"Wow! This is your piano. Can I touch it?" Peter ran over and stood next to it, caressing the wood with his fingertips.

"Yeah, that ol' beast is why I am living in this old hospital. I couldn't find a house with a big enough room or door to get it in. This place is owned by a friend of mine. There's a huge freight door over there where I was able to get a whole moving crew to drag it in here."

"There's a lot of history in this building. I never knew it was even here," Anne said.

"Yeah, I didn't either, but I got this piano as a gift, and I was freaking out about where I could move it too. As luck would have it, I have an old friend in construction who had acquired this property. He was going to restore it into a bed and breakfast, but it's a bloody money pit. He said I could just squat here rent-free if I kept an eye on the place.

He updated some of the plumbing and remodeled the kitchen for me, but everything else is original. The electricity was the first kind they installed back in the late-eighteen hundreds. It's so old, that it barely works, so I have these candles everywhere for when I lose power." Exa pointed to the candles littering the room.

"I thought you set them there to add to the ambiance," Anne said.

"They do make it beautiful, but no, unfortunately they are there because they are functional," Exa chuckled. "I don't know how much more he wants to invest in this dump, or even how long I will stay here." Exa's eyes glazed over as she scanned the room herself.

"Yeah, it has potential," Anne said. "This is gorgeous too." Anne pointed to a Victorian mirror hanging on the wall in front of the piano.

"Yeah, I think that's original too. I can't believe it's survived in the condition it's in. I love it hanging there because it gives me a view of my form when I play."

"It seems so timeless, standing here and knowing that it has been hanging here for so long. What a wonderful project – to restore this place," Anne said.

"Maybe for people who insist on preserving the past. I think somethings are better off left in the past," Exa said as she blinked her eyes, refocused her attention, and turned to Peter. "So anyway, Pe ta, you're a charming little boy. I hear you can play the piano. I know you didn't come here to see my hospital house so let's hear it."

Peter looked at the piano and self-consciously asked, "What do I play?"

"What do you know?" Exa asked.

"I just know songs when other people play them for me."

"I heard you could play by ear. Would you like me to play something and see how you do playing by ear?"

"Yeah, do that," Peter said.

"Okay, let's start with something easy. Umm, how about "Twinkle, Twinkle, Little Star"?" Exa talked to herself as she started to play the nursery rhyme from memory. Peter soaked up the sounds. He rubbed his finger joints to loosen them up while he waited. "You try it now," Exa said as she moved over on the bench and patted the spot next to her for Peter to sit.

Anne sat across the room with Shiloh's car seat at her feet. She was excited as she watched Peter huddle over the piano. He played the song as perfectly as Exa had done and finished with an enormous grin on his face. Exa's face never cracked. She looked at him for a second, and then played another song, a little bit harder one. Peter took a turn again and played it perfectly. They did this pattern of taking turns for a few more songs, and Exa never uttered a word. She just studied Peter's every move.

After Peter finished a fairly hard song perfectly, Exa got off the bench, walked over to the window, and looked outside for a few minutes. The room felt colder in the silence. Anne pulled Shiloh's blanket up tighter around him, waiting for Exa to say something.

Exa left the window and walked back to the piano, took a pack of cigarettes off the cover, lit one up, and took a slow drag – still not talking. Anne was thinking, *Who smokes in the house anymore around kids?* She was polite though and waited for Exa to finish her smoke.

Exa took another drag and flicked its' remnant into the fire place, she turned towards Anne and spoke frankly, "I'm no teacher. I don't really like kids, but can you come next Monday?"

"Yes," Anne was unable to mutter any other words as she was stunned by the offer. She wasn't sure what the offer was, but she wanted to help Peter. Mrs. Polly had assured her that Exa could help him.

"Okay, same time," Exa stated as she strode to the front door and opened it, motioning to Anne it was time for them to leave. Anne hurriedly stuffed Peter's feet into his boots, and threw his jacket on as the tone in the room felt sort of awkward. She grabbed Peter's arm and Shiloh's seat and hurried out, "Thank you. Should I call ahead next time?"

"Same time. Just be here," Exa stated, shutting the door briskly behind them.

Anne was confused. *Exa was friendly and talkative when we first arrived, but now she practically pushed us out the door.* She didn't know what to do so she just led her boys to the van and went home, waiting for next Monday.

The rest of the week went surprisingly smoothly. Peter was in a more tranquil mood unlike his normal, restless self. To everyone's surprise, he even slept through the night Monday. He spoke about Exa's piano and their session nonstop. Thomas was even optimistic about the sessions after he heard how excited Peter had been about them.

"So, does she give lessons?" Thomas questioned as he brushed his teeth with Anne that night.

"No, I don't think so. I mean, she flat out said she isn't a music teacher. I think she's just doing Mrs. Polly a favor. I don't know . . .; it was a weird meeting," Anne squeezed out a neat row of green toothpaste on her purple, glittered brush and handed the tube to Thomas.

"Weird how?" he questioned as he plopped a glob onto his brush and ran it under the water. He stepped back, so Anne, who was a lot shorter, could see into the mirror.

"I don't know how to explain it. Exa seems like she would be one of those people who's really eccentric. Maybe I just can't read her. I mean, she lives in this hospital. There's no furniture, except for the largest piano you've ever seen." Anne laughed as she ran a slow stream of water over her brush. "The electricity's unreliable, so she functions on sunlight and candles. I don't know how she cooks or if she does. It's like she just wants to hide out somewhere." Anne shut the water off, but held her brush steady in front of her. "She's also sort of moody. One minute she was talking and smiling and the next minute she was mute and chain smoking."

"Sounds li'e a trooue artist to meh," Thomas words sputtered out from the foaming paste in his mouth.

"Yeah, maybe. I don't know. I just know Peter was a different kid this week. He had a glow to him. I think this music stuff helps." Anne watched Thomas in the mirror.

"Yeah, maybe this is a good extra-curricular thing for him, since he's staying home for school now." Thomas had finished brushing and was now wiping his face off with a towel. Looking to Anne, he placed his hand on her waist. "Don't over think it. It's just toothpaste," he smiled at her in the mirror as he pointed to her unused toothpaste. He kissed the top of her head and exited the bathroom door.

"Maybe," Anne sighed as she still tried to figure it all out in her head and finally put the toothbrush in her mouth to brush.

Fifteen

Still remembering the past, Anne recalled she had stopped at the Steep & Brew on the way over to Exa's to pick up a round of drinks to help kick off their second session. Peter was over the moon-excited to see Exa's piano again. Exa smiled when they arrived, and she thanked Anne for the coffee. Exa was dressed in all black. Again. Anne tried to remember if it was the exact same black dress Exa had worn all three times they had met.

"Ah Pe ta, come inside. How was your week?"

"Awesome! I can't wait to play your piano again."

"Well, have a seat then," she said as she motioned to Peter to go over to the piano bench. "What moves you today?" she said as she came around and sat on the other side of the bench.

"What?" Peter wrinkled his nose.

"What do you want to play?" Her blue eyes sparkled.

"You pick."

"Okay, how about something classic? Let's try a Beethoven concerto. You cannot be a pianist and not know Beethoven."

"Sure," Peter replied.

"This is going to be harder. I don't expect you to play this by ear, but I want to see if you can pick it apart at all. It is *Beethoven's 5th Concert in E flat*, so that means you'll start with this key." She scooted over slightly to center herself. "Come sit right next to me and watch my hands," she added.

Peter obeyed and scooted over next to her; Anne and Shiloh took their seats by the window sill across the room. Exa flexed her fingers and began to play. The piece took a long time, but Peter never got restless. When she was finished, Exa turned, so she could see Anne, too. "What do you think about Mr. Beethoven?" she asked.

"I always thought classical music was so old school, but I've never heard anything like that in person. It was breathtaking," Anne said.

"Pe ta, did you like it?" Exa asked.

He nodded his head. "Do you think I can play that?"

"You'll probably have to work up to that, but I wanted you to hear what's possible. If you study piano, you can play beautiful concertos like that. Part of being a student of piano is just listening to other people play."

"Hearing it just makes me want to try to play it." Peter's eyes darted across the keys.

Exa turned to Anne, "I never wanted to be a teacher, but this is sort of fun to see. When you live your life as a musician, sometimes, you forget to marvel at it." She turned back to look at Peter. "It's refreshing to rediscover it through your eyes, Pe ta."

"We're so appreciative of your time, Exa. This has been fascinating for both of us," Anne said as she rocked Shiloh's car seat on the floor with her foot; little baby gurgles flowed from Shiloh's chair.

"Well, I don't have tons of time today. Would you like to play a quick song before you go or do you want me to play another song? Exa asked Peter as she turned back to face him.

"You can play another one. I'll listen," Peter said.

"Okay, um, this is one of my ALL-TIME favorites. I think I've played it almost every day since I was in high school. It's sort of how I wind down at the end of the day. It was also my wedding song."

"I didn't know you are married," Anne said.

"Yes, I am. My husband, Ambrose, is in Europe right now. We're both in the entertainment biz, so most of the time we are on opposite sides of the globe," Exa sighed, refocusing on the keys in front of her. "So, this one is Pachelbel, "Canon in D"."

"Oh, I know this one. It's so pretty," Anne said.

"It's like my theme song," Exa added as she positioned her hands to play the first chord. She closed her eyes and only opened them after the first few chords were out. Even with her eyes open, she didn't look at the keys. Instead, she appeared to be looking past the keys -- into her memory.

Anne couldn't decide who was more entertaining to watch, Exa or Peter. Peter let his jaw drop slightly as he watched Exa's hands flow across the keys. Anne noticed Peter's facial expression changing. His eyebrows tightened and his jaw clinched. Slowly the color drained from his face. Confused, Anne searched the room for something that was bothering him: only the music filled the room. Peter's shoulders shook. Anne stood, walked closer to Peter, and touched his arm.

Peter placed his hand on Exa's shoulder, motioning her to stop – thus she did. Looking at Peter, Anne asked, "What's wrong honey, are you okay?"

Peter pushed his hand into Exa's shoulder, he almost shouted, "I know it, I know it!"

Exa stared at Peter, confused by his random behavior.

"Exa, I know it! Can you move?" He said louder. Exa obliged, got up quickly, and looked to Anne for help. Anne scooted in next to Peter's side and reached her hand out to touch his arm again. Peter pushed her away.

Peter slid over on the piano bench, and in a moment so fast no one including Peter knew what was happening, Peter played the piano. Exa knew what he was playing as he picked up "Canon in D" exactly where she had left off. He continued playing it to perfection, just as if it were Exa playing it.

Peter chanted in a whisper all the while he played, "I know it. I know it." Peter finished playing the song, but let his fingers linger on the keys. "I know it. It's in my dreams."

Alarmed by his emotional outburst, Anne said in a voice barely above a whisper, "Peter, you're okay."

"Mom, that's the song from my dreams. I know it."

"You heard that song before in your dreams?"

"Yeah, all the time. It's before the Goat Woman comes after me."

"Well, maybe that explains why you knew how to play it?" Anne looked to Exa for help.

Exa spoke, "Peter, do you know what you just did?"

"Yeah, I played my dream song."

"Yeah . . . But, it wasn't playing by ear because you didn't hear it. You just played it from memory. That's impossible. Did you listen to this song somewhere else?"

"Yes, I told you. I heard it in my dreams."

Exa looked back at Anne and shrugged her shoulders, "I don't know. If I weren't sitting here when this happened, I would never have believed it. Even musical geniuses can't make up a song like that." Exa stood up and rubbed the back of her neck. "That's a lot to digest this early in the morning. I think we need a break." Anne ran her hand through her hair and nodded in agreement. "Where's that coffee that you brought me?" Exa asked before she spotted her lukewarm latte sitting on the piano. Grabbing it, she removed the lid, and drank half of it in a few huge gulps, like she was taking shots of booze.

Anne sat, pondering Peter's dreams explanation. This music thing was too complex for her to understand, but she was concerned about the emotions flooding out of Peter when he spoke about his dreams. This was the first she'd heard about a song.

"I don't think there's much more to do today after that." Exa half laughed as she came up for air from her latte. "I'm maxed out."

Anne tucked Shiloh's blanket in around him and then picked up his car seat, heading towards the door. Exa walked to the window again with a cigarette, and she started to flick a lighter. At first, Anne thought she should keep her mouth shut, but then she reconsidered. "Exa, I'm sorry to be a pain, and I hate to even ask . . . I really appreciate you letting us come to your home, but Peter has terrible lung issue because he was born prematurely. Do you mind waiting a few moments until after we step out the door to smoke? I just need Peter to get his shoes on, and we're gone."

Exa turned her head to look at Anne. Expressionless, she stared and then shook her head. She took her cigarette, flipped it into the fireplace, and sat down in front of it on the hearth, facing Anne. "I thought when my friend told me about him that I would see this kid who likes to bang on the piano or, maybe even better, someone who reminded me of myself. But Pe ta, I don't have the words for. I don't smoke. These were left here by one of the construction workers. I need to do something to fill my void of words," Exa rambled.

"I'm sorry, I shouldn't have said anything. I'm a bit of an over-protective mom." Anne was now embarrassed by her actions. She jammed Peter's foot into his shoe in an effort to hurry him along.

"You don't get it. You think you're bringing your child to some little music class to replace what he had in school?" Exa's voice was noticeably changing to an irritated tone.

"I'm not sure I know what you're asking. I thought you were alright with us visiting?" Anne backed slowly towards the door. She grabbed Peter's hand while she held Shiloh's car seat with the other hand.

"Just stop your crazy life for a minute and look at your kid!" Her boots clicked as she walked over to Peter and pointed a finger in his face. "This doesn't exist. It's impossible to do what he just did. That's not playing by ear; he never heard the song before. He has a talent nobody can even dream about. What the heck it is, I don't know."

Anne pulled Peter closer to her and nudged him toward the door. "I'm sorry to upset you. We're leaving now." She pushed Peter through the door. "Thank you for your time," she added before she pulled the door closed behind her.

"Yeah, you leave. I don't need this on my plate. I'm supposed to be on sabbatical, not playing with grade-schoolers," Exa called after them.

Anne was frightened by Exa's behavior, but even more than that, Peter's reaction to Exa and the fact that he played a song from memory, which was "impossible" frightened her even more.

After speeding down the street for a block, Anne pulled the van over to the side of the road to regroup. Shiloh had fallen asleep already and had a pleasant little baby grin on his face. In the rearview mirror, Anne observed Peter sitting in his car seat. He had made himself "invisible" by putting on his sunglasses. His flushed checks spoke the truth about his feelings.

Anne wanted to talk to Peter about what had happened at Exa's but she knew this wasn't the time. Anne argued internally with herself while drove home, *I have four other kids and together all of them added up do not equal the emotional stress and heartbreak this one kid gives me daily. He's unable to function at school with the rest of the kids his age, but somehow, from somewhere, he has this amazing talent. Did that just really happen? How can he do that?*

When Anne pulled into the driveway, she noticed Thomas's truck, which was unusual for a mid-morning weekday. Her heart skipped a beat as her mind flashed scenarios of why he would be home. She didn't think Peter, nor she, could handle any more drama this morning.

Anne grabbed her purse and Shiloh's car seat and ushered Peter into the house. She found Thomas in the kitchen. "You're home?" She arched her eyebrows.

His brown eyes were vibrant and sparkling, which was a good sign. "Yeah, I have a surprise for Peter." He glanced at Peter, who was still wearing his sunglasses of invisibility. "Where's Peter?" he asked.

Anne pursed her lips in a pause before she finally said, "We went to Exa's, and he had a really great lesson. He played Pachelbel's "Canon in D" – like he played it without hearing it – the whole thing, perfectly." Anne paused again to make sure Thomas was listening. He had remained silent. Anne continued, "You know that song they sometimes use for weddings that goes like do do do do dooo? Peter played it. He knows it from somewhere."

"He learned it before?"

"No, that's just it. He'd never played it before. He literally had a meltdown when Exa started playing it. He said he heard it in his Goat Woman dreams." Anne's eyes opened wide, showing Thomas how confused she was with the situation. "He forced her away from the piano so he could finish the piece. Then, Exa got freaked out; she starting yelling at Peter, telling him that it was impossible for him to do what he had just done."

"She yelled. Like she scolded him?"

"No, not scolding, but she was visibly upset. It scared Peter; she scared me, but then she made me think about it. She said, 'it's impossible for him to play a piece like that', especially without ever having heard it. So, something's going on with him. How can he do that?"

Thomas was always careful to speak, especially when it involved Peter. He scratched his chin. After a few moments, he said, "Peter's always been a special kid. We knew *that* Anne from the moment we met him. If this is his gift, then who are we to question it? If this is what makes him special, then we have an obligation to help him pursue it."

Anne nodded tearfully. "I'm in awe of how he can just do this, but at the same time, it's so hard, Thomas. The other kids are so easy. I just drop them off at school, and they make good grades; they have friends and don't require too much fuss. With Peter, I just don't know if I'm doing enough."

Thomas reached his arms out, wrapped them around Anne, and pulled her in close to him, resting his chin on top of her head. "I know. He's the best part of us." He bent down to kiss the tip of her nose. "So... can we handle this surprise now or do you think we should wait?"

"It depends on what it is? A European woman to give us piano lessons, no thanks," she joked as she wiped her unfallen tears out of her eyes with her sleeve.

"Come on. I think I've got the perfect thing to make Peter visible again." Thomas walked to the end of the hallway and yelled, "Peter, I've got a surprise for you!" No response. "Peter! It's a really cool surprise, and it's also a secret I want to show you."

Little footsteps shuffled around from inside his room and then, Peter peeked around the door. Still invisible, Peter made no attempt to talk, but he was curious. He crossed the hall and stopped just short of the kitchen doorway.

"This is a HUGE surprise. I couldn't fit it in the house." Thomas held his arms opened all the way apart to show how large the surprise is. "We have to trudge through the snow, so put your snow boots on."

Anne looked toward Thomas. "I don't want to miss a surprise that we have to go snowshoeing for. I'm going get Shiloh bundled up."

A few moments later, they clumsily traipsed through the snow in the backyard. There was already a trail, with several sets of steps, leading to the old, detached garage in the backyard. The garage sat at the end of the lot next to the alley; it was the original one built for the house. After the Arnold's bought the house, they added an attached garage when they remodeled the kitchen. The old garage was never shoveled out after it snowed. It was mostly filled with storage items and one, not even close to being restored, baby blue, 1957, Chevy convertible.

For dramatic effect, Thomas paused before getting to the door. He smiled and asked, "Are you ready, Peter Arnold?" Still invisible, Peter never said a word. "Anne, I want to show Peter my surprise, but I can't see him. Do you know if he's here with us?"

"I don't know. I thought I heard something, but you know when he goes invisible, it's so hard to know what he's doing. Peter, if you are here can you show yourself?"

Smiling timidly, Peter pulled his glasses halfway down his nose, pausing for a second, and then taking them all the way off. "Yeah I'm here. I want to see it."

"Great! Everybody get ready for the surprise . . . tada!" Thomas whipped open the door, revealing a dark, musty garage cluttered up with so many boxes it was hard to see exactly what the surprise was. "Okay here, come closer." Thomas flipped on the light switch and waved for them to follow him inside. Anne went in first and was met with a warm wave of air, which she found odd, until she noticed a heater attached to the corner ceiling that was never there before.

Peter's excitement caused him to forget he was upset; he inched closer. Anne strained her eyes to adjust to the darker light after having been in the snowy brightness; the surprise manifested for both Anne and Peter at the same time. "Thomas! You didn't?"

"A piano!" Peter ran to his new gift.

"It's the piano from the children's wing of the hospital. It was going to the dump to make room for a computer desk if I didn't rescue it. I had a couple of the janitors help me bring it over. I didn't even want to try to put it in the house." Thomas ran his hand along the wall that had previously been unfinished, framed beams, but was now sheet rocked, textured, and painted. "I hired our maintenance guys to finish the garage into a studio for you. It didn't take much to install that garage heater," Thomas said as he pointed to the heater. "We don't use this space for anything anyway. Peter, you can play out here whenever you want, and then it won't bother Shiloh." Thomas's smile shown through his brown eyes. "Do you like it, Bud?"

Peter jumped up and down with excitement. "Can I play you my song?"

"Your solo?" Thomas asked.

"No, my dream song."

Anne swallowed hard and whispered to Thomas, "That's "Canon in D". He said he knows it because it was in his dreams." Anne didn't want Peter to get emotional all over again. She elbowed Thomas.

"Sure, I would love to hear it," Thomas said. Anne held her breath, afraid of his reaction, and worried he would play the song exactly like he did before, perfectly.

Peter sat on the old bench; it squeaked and wobbled as he got comfortable. He pushed a few of the keys to test them. The sound hung in the air.

"It sounds like it still works well," Anne said.

"I'll get someone over here to tune it, but it's fine for now," Thomas said as he looked at Peter, "Play."

Peter leaned into the keys and singular chords bridged together into a melody filling the brisk air. The piece of music was just as recognizable as before. However, this time, Anne kept her eye on Thomas.

Peter finished the song with a big smile. "Can I really keep this piano?"

Thomas nodded, "I think the piano wants to know if it can keep you. That was beautiful Peter."

Now, it was Anne's turn to freak out. "Thomas, Peter just played this song. He didn't learn it. He never practiced it. He said he had heard it in a dream. Does this happen?"

Both Peter and Thomas stared at Anne. Thomas said, "It just did." He held out his hand for Peter to join him. "Come on son, its cold. Let's go get some hot chocolate before I have to go back to work soon."

"Ah!" Anne grunted as she watched her family go back toward the house. Ironically now she understood Exa's outburst. It was the frustration of seeing something so awesome and unbelievable when you are used to living in a world with explanations. "Wait for me and Shiloh!"

When they did not oblige her, she took matters into her own hands — snowball style. It had been years since Anne rolled a big fat snow ball, but she hadn't forgotten how to pack it just perfectly. She launched it as hard as she could, smacking Thomas on the side of his head and taking him by surprise; he jumped on its impact. Anne felt great. *This is great stress relief.*

"You are so dead!" Thomas called as he turned around already packing his own ball. "Peter, get your mom! She's attacking us!"

"I have Shiloh. You can't throw snow at Shiloh!" Anne called back as she ran toward the house with the baby.

"I have great aim." Thomas blasted a ball that hit Anne's leg hard.

"Ouch! Okay, we're even. We each got one."

"Take this, mom!" Peter whizzed a ball through the air, plopping it right on Anne's back side; she was impressed.

"Nice throw, Peter. But, can you catch?" She launched one back, but it fell apart before it could hit him. Peter giggled.

"Okay family, truce. Let's go inside," Anne said. They all agreed. It was fun to throw snowballs, but they hurt when you get hit. "I feel better now," Anne sighed. The boys laughed.

Sixteen

Continuing with her earlier memories about Exa, Anne recalled how several weeks had passed after Exa kicked Anne and the boys out of her house. Each day, Thomas went to work, and Tane, Paul, and Marie went to school. Anne taught Peter his lessons at home as she carried Shiloh in a sling to keep him quiet and happy. In the afternoon, Peter would venture out to the garage to play his piano.

Many nights, Anne lay awake thinking about all the "Should I's" when it came to parenting Peter. She was convinced homeschooling was the best way to educate him, and she was content in most of her decisions but one; Exa Scarletta. Something about Exa lingered in Anne's mind. It wasn't just the outburst and the moodiness, but there was something familiar about her that Anne was yet to put her finger on. She tried to push it out of her head, but it must've been bothering Exa too because out of the blue, Exa called her. "Hi Anne. It's Exa. Don't hang up."

"I won't. Hi."

"Anne, I'm not sure why I'm calling. I guess, I feel I owe you and Pe ta an apology. I'm sorry. I didn't mean to scare Pe ta or to be mean."

"Don't worry about it. I had an outburst almost like yours later that night when I tried to explain to my husband what was going on."

"That makes me feel better. I just kept thinking that you thought terrible things about me, but I was really confused. I can't stop thinking about Pe ta. I've been doing some research and been hearing some stories sort of like Pe ta's."

"Really? Like what?"

"Well, nothing exactly like his, but along the same line. I've learned something interesting; apparently, researchers believe every single song you hear is stored permanently in the subconscious, and sometimes it can be triggered into your current memory."

"Hmm, really?"

"Yeah, part of your brain holds memories that you don't normally have access too. I guess some people are more sensitive to triggers that can help them access it."

"Okay. . ."

"So get this . . . I was mentioning this to a friend when we were at a charity event, and there was this music director there. He said he once went to see a concert and the director was his good friend but his friend had gotten sick during the show. He had the flu and was literally vomiting nonstop. At intermission, his friend asked him to step in as the conductor to finish the show.

This director knew most of the songs on the program, so he said he would try. The band was well rehearsed, so he knew they could get through it – even though he was a novice with some of the songs. Once he started, things went well, and then the band were going to play this piece he had never worked on before. He had decided to start them off, and then stand back and let them work their way through it. When the band started to play, something inside of him switched, and he knew every note and directed it perfectly. He was shocked and unable to explain how he knew it.

He called his mother, who was also a musician, I think he said she played the cello . . . anyway that doesn't really matter. She asked what piece it was, and he told her. She said she knew it because it was the song she had been working on when she was pregnant with him. They joked about how he must have been listening, *but* I guess, since then, he has done some research on his own, and he believes the song was stored in his subconscious from pregnancy. That's how he knew it and hearing it had triggered it."

Anne was silent. "Anne, are you still there?"

Sighing, "Yeah I'm here. I don't know if I can believe that's what happened with Peter."

"Yeah, I wouldn't have believed it either if I hadn't seen what happened with Peter. Can you give me a better explanation? I guess music is one of those things that stays in the brain forever. So Pe Ta could have heard that song anywhere and the memory was just triggered. Pachelbel is popular. You said you heard it before. Peter was probably with you and, somehow, he stored it."

"I can't... I guess, your explanation is the best we have so far. So, you believe he heard the song before, that it was stored in his brain, and it just popped out?"

"I don't know what I believe, but it's a possible explanation for an unexplainable scenario." After a long pause, Exa continued, "Anne, what do you want to do?"

"Do I have to do anything? He's a kid." Anne looked at the clock and saw it was almost time to start dinner. She walked over to the kitchen sink and tucked the phone between her chin and shoulder to free her hands. She started pulling dirty dishes from the sink and placed them into the dishwasher; she could never cook in a messy kitchen.

"You're the mom, but I just feel like this needs to be explored a little more," Exa said softly.

"Why? So, we explore it a little more, and then he plays some more music. What does it matter?" Anne pulled the top rack of the dishwasher out to stack the glasses. One glass had curdled milk in the bottom. Anne gagged as she scrubbed it out and ran it under rinse water.

"It matters because your son has a gift. He's a musical genius. Don't you think you should help him explore it?"

"He's playing the piano every day. You said there's no point in lessons; what else is there?"

"A career, Anne. Your son could have a career."

"Career?" Anne snorted. "He's in kindergarten." Anne folded the dishwasher door up with her foot as she gripped the phone with one hand, shutting the running water off with the other one.

"Anne, I'm going to be honest with you because you have trouble facing reality. I could call my manager tomorrow, tell him about Peter, and, within a few weeks, Peter could be famous. Heck, in this world, he doesn't even need organized management, we could put a video out on the Internet; this kid would become famous."

"Famous. I don't think we need any fame." Anne ran a rag under warm water and rung it out.

"Anne, you have a talented son. You can help him to share his talent. He could have a career most people would die for. Or, you can run from it, and he could spend the rest of his life struggling to be happy, selling used cars or working at a bank."

"He's 6-years-old," Anne said flatly as she wiped counters, and then leaned against the kitchen wall. Her bangs had fallen flat against her forehead from the steam of the hot water she used to rinse the dishes. She tried sweeping her hair out of her face, but failed.

"Talent knows no age. Sometimes, young artists have an advantage because they have a unique image."

"Exa, please don't be offended, but my son doesn't need a career. He's fine. If he's so talented, then this career thing will be there for him when he graduates."

"Maybe, but I won't be."

"What do you have to do with it?" Anne wiped her sticky bangs again, pushing them to the side.

"Nothing I guess. I was just thinking about how nice it would have been for me to have a mentor in this industry. There are a lot of ways you can make mistakes in this business."

"So, what are you saying? You want to mentor him."

"Maybe, if he wants to just come around and hang out; he can learn some of the business. I mean, you and he can come around, and you both can learn."

"This is really overwhelming, Exa. I mean, I'm amazed at Peter's talent, but I don't think he needs to learn a business at his age."

"I know. I don't mean business like that, but just to get some early exposure. Please talk to your husband, and think about it. I've tried not to think about Pe ta these last few weeks, but I can't. So... this is what I'm offering."

"I guess, we can think about it."

"Sounds good. Would you like to bring Pe ta by tomorrow morning?"

"I can ask him."

"Anne, you're doing the right thing. I wish my mother had seen my talent when I was young and helped me learn about the industry. She ignored it and thought I was just like everyone else with a dead-end dream. It was frustrating; it put a lot of distance between us. As soon as I was eighteen, I ran away from home to Chicago. I was desperate for opportunity, and I had a lot to learn; I made a lot of bad choices. I think it's better if you start learning about it now. Even if you don't do anything, you can learn about it, so the opportunity is there if Pe ta does want it later."

"Well, right now, the only thing I'm focused on is getting him through kindergarten. However, if you're your willing to help him, I'm not going to say no. If you say it can help, then we'll try."

"I do. Anne, I really do."

"Okay, bye."

"Bye."

"Who was that?" Thomas asked as he walked by Anne to grab a bottle of water from the refrigerator.

"Exa."

He turned around. "What? Pipe smoking Exa?" Thomas teased as he faked smoking a pipe.

"Shut up, it wasn't a pipe, you dork." Anne laughed as she flung a dish towel at him. "Yeah, she apologized. She said her behavior was bugging her, and she offered to keep seeing Peter as a mentor."

"I thought she said she couldn't teach him anything?" Thomas took a swig of water, put the lid back on, and set it on the counter.

"No, she was talking about helping him learn the industry."

"The industry. He's a kindergartner," Thomas chuckled.

"Yeah, that's what I said. I don't know. According to her, he has this great talent. She said it was fine to wait until he was older to decide for himself, but we should at least learn as much as we can now to help him, so we are educated if that time comes."

"So, can I ask a question, Anne? Why does she care about our son? I thought she was this super-famous piano Goddess?" Thomas opened the pantry door and started rummaging through it.

"I really don't know. I think she's surprised that she cares. I think she thought she would see him once as a favor to Mrs. Polly, and then she would smile, and say, 'Wow you are great, keep practicing'. She never expected to see what she saw, none of us did. She sees this talented kid, who she's afraid will get taken advantage of if he ever tries to tap into the industry." Anne stood next to Thomas, who had removed several half-empty snack boxes from the shelves of the pantry and was trying to balance them in his hands. "What are you looking for? I got some more of that cheesy popcorn."

"I don't know. Maybe I'm just bored, but I want a something crunchy, and I don't buy this whole Exa thing either."

Anne glared at him. "What do you mean?"

"It just seems odd she would do all this. Did she say what her time is going to cost?" Thomas opened a bag of stick pretzels and took a few. "Oh, these are stale. Blah." Thomas quickly swallowed them and reached for his water bottle as he chucked the pretzels into the garbage.

"No, she never said she wanted any money." Anne closed the garbage lid that Thomas left open.

"Anne, are you really this naive? Maybe she's one of the people in the "Industry" we should be leery of?"

Anne crossed her arms. "I don't think so. In a strange way, I trust her. Most people who have something to hide don't open their house to you. I'm more worried about if Peter can handle it with his hands and weak immune system."

Thomas leaned against the fridge, still holding his water bottle. "As far as Peter's health is concerned, just take it one day at a time. But, the bigger issue is I don't think Mrs. Piano Goddess is being honest. Maybe, she is trying to exploit Peter for her gain?"

"I don't think so, and she's not a piano goddess so stop calling her that."

"Um, have you Googled this Exa chick? You don't listen to classical music, so you have not heard of her, but she's the ultimate piano Goddess in her world."

"Well, if she's so famous, why is she here hanging out with us?" Anne's forehead wrinkled.

"Exactly my point."

"Well, now what? I still want to see her tomorrow."

"She invited you over?"

"Yeah, I'm think I'm already getting excited for Peter. I want to see where this road leads him." Anne nervously chewed off her pinky nail on her left hand.

"Go if you want, but I would not, under any circumstances, let her be unsupervised with Peter. I think we need to proceed cautiously. You can't trust everyone." Thomas finished his water bottled and threw it in the trash before he walked out of the kitchen. Anne reached over to close the garbage can lid again.

Seventeen

Anne had given Exa one more chance and it turned out to be the start of a long mentorship for Peter and Anne with Shiloh by her side. They tried to meet once a week; it didn't always work out, but the visits added variety to their homeschool week. There was never personal talk or even much talking at all. Exa never asked for any money, and when Anne offered, Exa appeared offended, so she didn't bring it up again.

Time flew by quickly, and soon spring was upon them. Peter had finished up his schooling a few weeks before his siblings did. He occupied himself in the garage, playing the piano, and he was never happier. His personality blossomed into a more settled, less fearful child. Piano was his entertainment, his stress reliever, his self-expression, and his friend. Peter had finally found *his place* in the world.

The household was running smoothly until Thomas dropped a bomb on Anne, telling her that he took a job overseas for the summer. "You have to leave for how long?" Anne's eyes were wide open as she glared at Thomas.

"Twelve weeks," Thomas said flatly.

"That's the whole summer." Anne's face froze as she mentally converted the weeks into months.

"Yeah, I guess if you look at it that way," Thomas said.

"The hospital's okay with this?" Anne's eyes bounced around Thomas's face looking for a sign that he was joking.

"Yeah, they're the ones who recommended me for the job; it's good publicity for them."

"Is it safe?" Anne felt her cheeks getting warm.

"It's Tanzania. It's a third-world country, but I'll be staying at the mission house. There's a lot of American's working there." Thomas casually flipped through the T.V. Guide on the kitchen island.

"Are you sure you want this job?" Anne was still in disbelief.

"I do. It isn't glamorous by any means, but they need good doctors who are willing to donate some time. I know I can do a good job."

"Donate?" Anne's eyebrow arched.

"Yeah, I'll be donating my time. The mission will pay for my plane ticket and my room and board, but my time's going to be donated." Thomas lifted one corner of his mouth is a half-smile as he starred at Anne.

"You're going to work for free. Can we afford that?"

"I don't leave until the end of May. I can moonlight in the ER for some overtime pay before I go. We'll have to scrimp, but it'll work out."

"Okay, let me get this straight." Anne held a finger up in the air while she spoke, "You're leaving in four weeks for twelve weeks. Until you leave, you're going to work nonstop to make extra money, so we won't see you. Then, you leave me here all summer with five kids and no money to entertain them?"

"It's not that bad. We'll have money. Nothing will change. Can you afford any major purchases? Not now, but we'll be fine." Annoyed, Thomas flipped the T.V. Guide closed, and tossed it onto a pile of mail at the end of the island.

"Thomas, what about my sanity?" Anne crossed her arms in front of her.

"Come on now, it's not like I am going to be staying at the Ritz. I'm going to be in a third- world country." Thomas mirrored Anne's stance by crossing his arms.

"Yeah, but you chose this."

"You chose it, too. You knew when we got married that I wanted to be a doctor. You were well aware of the sacrifices that would come with it." Thomas waved his finger towards Anne as he spoke.

"Yeah, in *America*. I didn't plan on you leaving for twelve weeks when I have a five-month-old and four other kids. When you get back, Shiloh will be almost nine months old. He won't even know you."

"Oh, that's enough with the guilt trip, Anne. Most people would be proud of their husbands for going on a mission like this." Thomas paced to the other side of the room opposite Anne.

Anne got quiet and paused before she spoke again, "I'm proud of you, but sometimes it feels like you make decisions on what's best for you, not what's best for our whole family. I just had a baby; we have five kids; I need help," Anne weakly whispered the last sentence.

Thomas's brown eyes softened. "I know. Well, maybe we can hire a part-time mother's helper?"

"With what money? I know what's in the bank account. It'll barely cover the house payment and my van payment for the next three months. How we're going to eat is beyond me."

"I said, I will work overtime to get some money in the account."

"So, this your final decision then? I don't really get a say? You're telling me this is the way it is going to be," Anne asked coldly.

"Anne, I need to do this. Don't be mad at me."

"Okay, then. Maybe I'll have to get a part-time job this summer, so my kids can eat because my husband is off volunteering." *I really think you are trying to kill me or at least drive me insane,* she thought.

"Anne, it's not like that."

"Mom, Dad, what are you guys yelling about?" Marie interrupted as she walked into the kitchen. "You two sound like Tane and Paul."

"It's nothing. Just grown-up stuff," Thomas said.

"It's nothing?" Anne huffed. "Leaving your kids for the whole summer is nothing?"

"What, dad? You're leaving?" Marie asked.

"Anne, now is not the time to blurt this out," Thomas yelled.

"When is the time?" Anne asked.

"Dad, is it true?" Marie pressed.

Defeated, Thomas glared at Anne and sighed, "Yes, it's true. Your mom's obviously upset at me, so she's making a big deal about it. I wanted to wait to tell you and your brother's all at once, but yes, I'm taking a job with a medical mission overseas for the summer. I'll be able to help a lot of people who wouldn't have access to a doctor without me there."

"I don't want you to leave," Marie cried.

"I told you. This isn't going to be easy," Anne huffed.

"Paul, Tane, Peter! Dad's leaving for the whole summer! Come tell him not to go!" Marie yelled.

"Marie! Shh! Let's not get everyone upset right this minute," Thomas said.

"Why not? Because it makes you uncomfortable, and you would rather wait until it's just me here to deal with it?" Anne asked.

"What has gotten into you, Anne?" Thomas asked. "You're becoming so cynical. You never used to be like this."

"What has gotten into me? This has been the hardest year of my life, Thomas. I had school problems every day for half the year when I was *pregnant and sick*. Then, I gave birth to a baby and had to start homeschooling Peter at the same time. I get, maybe, 4 hours of sleep a night and that's not in a row. I don't know what I'm doing. I have five kids to raise all by myself because you're barely home, and now, you're making your absence official by leaving for a solid twelve weeks! Don't I get a say?"

The rest of the kids had filed into the kitchen and heard every word of Anne's rant. The kids were all shouting questions for Thomas about his leaving them. The noise level was through the roof, even Shiloh was protesting.

"Enough! Everybody shut your mouths!" Thomas roared. "See what happens to the kids when you get all upset Anne?"

"They're upset because you're leaving. Don't put this on me!"

"Stop," Peter yelled with his hands over his ears. "Stop it. You tell us to talk to each other in loving ways. Stop it."

Peter's innocence made Anne feel like a fool. Now ashamed, but still overwhelmed at the thought of Thomas leaving for the whole summer, Anne shrugged her shoulders as she looked to Thomas, who broke the silence, trying to shed some light on the discussion. "Kids, yes, I'll be gone all summer. I have to help people who need a doctor. You'll all be here together, and you'll have a fun summer; I promise. It'll fly by and when I get back, we'll try to do something really special together . . . maybe a camping trip."

The idea of a camping trip was enough to distract Tane and Paul. Marie was still upset because she wanted to go, too. Anne fumed inside, but tried to hide it. *I love my kids immensely. I'm fortunate to have some wonderful kids, and I try to take all the daily stress one day at a time, however, this huge chunk of time without any backup is going to test me beyond all my limits. I'm going to go crazy!*

Things weren't settled though. The kids didn't calm down and Thomas couldn't shake how badly he felt for leaving Anne and the stress he was causing her. So, unbeknownst to Anne, Thomas did some more planning, and the next day he had another idea.

"You're taking my daughter to a third-world country?" Anne repeated.

"Well, yes. But, it's to help you. Just hear me out. I asked my mom to come with us to help supervise Marie. Mom and Marie are going to work in the orphanage. They will fly back home together after the month is over."

"Marie's my helper. You're taking my last piece of sanity." Anne glared at Thomas.

Thomas held up a hand. "Just wait and listen. When my dad heard about their trip, he offered to take Tane and Paul to his cabin in Montana for a few weeks. They can ride the train out there and spend their time fishing, hiking, and doing whatever the boys want to do. So, you'll have one month with just the two kids. Paul and Tane will get to have a fun vacation, so they don't feel left out. Marie will get to do something interesting, too. Really, it'll work out."

"I can't not see my kids for a month," Anne said. "I've never been away from them."

"I know, but they're all excited. My dad really wants this time with the boys, and Marie was born to do this kind of work. Everyone will be back home by the beginning of July. My dad will cover the cost of feeding and housing the boys for a month. The money you save on groceries can be used to get Peter into swimming lessons, and you should have some extra fun money for when they all get back."

"They all want to go?" Anne asked. *I know the boys will have fun at the cabin. It will be nice for them to have some time with grandpa. And it will be good for Marie to do something like this. I can handle Peter and Shiloh by myself. . .*

"Yeah." Thomas nodded his head.

"I can't believe I'm going to say this, but alright, but only *if* they want to go. *This is insane. It's feels irresponsible to let my kids be gone, but yes, let the kids have a summer to remember.*" Anne was half heartbroken to be losing her kids for a month, but excited for them, too.

* * *

Back at the hospital, Thomas came to relieve Anne from Peter's bedside. It was now day three of Peter's ordeal, and Anne had stayed up most of the night reliving Peter's childhood in her head. Exhausted, but surviving, Anne did want to spend time with the twins this morning while Peter's condition remained unchanged.

She sped home in Thomas's truck. Back at home, even with the pitter-patter of two sets of kiddy feet, the house felt empty. Anne wasn't planning on staying long, so she tried to make the most of her time. She offered to go outside to play Frisbee. Both twins agreed, and even Shiloh, who had been babysitting them, offered to play, so the teams would be even.

In the backyard, Anne tried not to look at the garage, but she failed. It was so much a part of her life having to look back here constantly to see what Peter was up to. Half expecting to hear the piano as they fanned out over the backyard to form teams, Anne couldn't shake the memories. She could practically hear the piano chords flowing through the door. She stood next to the door forbidding herself to touch the door knob; she touched the trim next to it, running her fingers along the wood, careful not to get a splinter. The wood was rough and worn through the white finish as it was past the "gently used" stage and deserved a fresh coat of paint. Anne exhaled and closed her eyes. She could see Peter sitting at the piano with a huge, boyish grin on his face.

* * *

"What are you working on out here?" Anne, who was standing in the opened garage door, asked Peter, who was only five at the time.

"My song. I wrote it. Can I play it for you?" Peter looked back at her.

"Sure, I would love that."

"It's called, "The Goat Woman," Peter proudly stated.

A lump popped up in the back of Anne's throat. "The Goat Woman . . . that lady from your dreams?"

"Yeah," Peter nodded excitedly.

"I thought she was scary to you. Why would you write a song about her?"

"She is scary. But mom, she's not just in my dreams. I can't stop thinking about her, so when I started to write, this is what came out. It's how I feel when I think about her."

Anne gave up months ago on the whole Goat Woman topic. She had nothing to say about it as long as Peter wasn't having a meltdown over it; she just went with the flow. "Let me hear it." She leaned against the door frame, waiting to be entertained.

Anne didn't know anything about music except the little bit she heard at Exa's house and the stuff she heard coming from her garage. However, she felt she knew enough to know when something was at least worthy of being heard. As she listened to Peter's first original concerto, her heart pounded. *This is really creepy; it sounds like something from a Dracula movie.* Anne chewed on her lip while she listened, vowing to be supportive.

When Peter was done playing, Anne said, "That was great honey. I love it." She clapped.

"Thanks. I'm going to play it for Exa. She said she's working on an album. I want her to help me get this on my own album."

"Your own album. That's a pretty big dream."

"You always tell me to dream big."

"Yeah, I do say that. If you are going to bother to do something might as well do it big." Anne tried pushing aside Peter's preoccupation with the Goat Woman. *Don't think about the Goat Woman thing. It's just a phase like the boogie man,* Anne told herself. *A really long phase. It doesn't mean anything. . .*

At Peter's next session with Exa, he was ecstatic to play his concerto for Exa. He had to use the bathroom before he could get started. "Exa, I just started playing, and it came to me. I couldn't stop until I had all the chords out of my head," Peter explained as he positioned himself at her piano.

"Wow, I don't think I wrote my first concerto until I was in my twenties. You're ahead of the curve." Exa winked at Anne as they all waited patiently for him to play.

Peter giggled. "Yes, so I know this Goat Woman, and she's really scary. One time, I saw her, and she was all bloody. She saw me, and she was chasing me, but I got away. I wrote this about her," Peter said matter-of-factly. Exa laughed because she thought he was joking about his narrative, but then she saw Peter's face and stopped laughing; because he looked completely serious.

"Oh, that does sound scary," Exa retracted her laugh and replaced it with a straight face.

"Okay, I'm going to play now," Peter quipped. He pressed the keys with distinction. Anne heard the now familiar tune, but she enjoyed watching Exa's expression. Nothing about Peter's talent ever got old to either one of them. Anne had a load of mother's pride wrapped around Peter, but Exa felt passion for the music. When it was over, Peter was apprehensive to hear Exa's critique.

Exa took a minute to respond, needing to live in the moment for a minute to really connect to what she had just heard. After several moments passed, without words, Exa nodded her head. Pe ta, that was. . . that was really great."

"Thanks," Peter said.

"I mean it, Pe ta. You're a natural talent. I hope you know it. Someday, I'll see your name in lights at Madison Square Garden or maybe Radio City Music Hall. I'll be so proud to know you." Exa's voice was squeaky.

"Exa, are you okay? Do you need some water?" Anne asked.

"No water, thank you though." Exa cleared her throat.

"So, I didn't think this would be hard, but for some reason I feel stuck." Exa took a deep breath. "But, I'm going to be leaving on tour in two weeks. After the tour, I plan to go to Europe to spend some time with my husband. I don't plan on coming back here. This needs to be our last session. I have so much to do before I leave . . ." Her voice trailed off as she spoke. Peter's face turned from glowing to pale, and then to flush red.

Anne wrapped an arm around Peter and pulled him close. "Well, that's not what we wanted to hear, but we know you have your career. Honestly, we never expected you to help us as much as you have. You mean the world to us both. Thank you so much for what you have done," Anne said.

"Yeah, don't mention it," Exa awkwardly smiled, avoiding eye contact. "You know, I thought I could teach Pe ta something, but it turns out I learned more from my sessions with Pe ta than he could ever learn from me. I appreciated this time together too." Exa, never an outwardly affectionate person, reached one arm over to give Peter a side hug. "I know Pe ta, you will have music in your life forever. Some people are just born to do something; you were born to be a piano master. When I was first asked to meet you, I thought I was doing you a favor, and you were lucky to meet a famous piano player. Now, I know, I'm the lucky one." Her words lingered sweetly within the sobering mood of the room.

"Why's everyone leaving?" Peter asked as he turned to his mom.

"I guess it's just life. People have to live their lives." Anne tried to answer as honestly as she could. She got up and walked Peter to the door and knelt in front of Peter to help him get his shoes on.

"Someone else is leaving?" Exa asked.

"Ah, temporarily, my husband's leaving for the summer. He took a temporary position in an underserved area in Tanzania. He's taking our daughter, and my other two boys are going to spend time with their grandpa," Anne said. She dug into her purse for her keys and picked up Shiloh's car seat.

"Wow, that sounds exciting for them," Exa said. "I bet you won't know what to do with yourself having three less kids."

"It will be an interesting summer. We will miss you." Anne looked up to meet Exa's gaze as she placed her free hand on Peter's shoulder, directing him toward the door.

"I'll miss you, too." Exa said softly as she clung to the open door.

"Well, if you are ever in the area, come back to visit us."

"I will." Exa nodded.

"Well, I guess this is goodbye."

"Yes, goodbye friends," Exa said.

Peter was silent.

The trio headed home to start their quiet summer. Anne was looking forward to a slower pace until, she received a phone call.

"Hello."

"Anne, it's Exa."

"Hi, how are you?"

"I'm well. I'm getting ready to leave on my tour. You're going to think I'm crazy, but I can't shake this feeling I have. I have to ask you something."

"What?"

"Is there anyway Pe ta can come with me? I mean Pe ta and you, or however it would work?"

"Come with you where?"

"On my tour. I know it sounds crazy, but I keep hearing Pe ta's song, and it's fantastic. I thought, what if he could open for me? He would be great. I really want to do this for him. You said your family was leaving for the summer and I just started to think it would make sense."

Anne was speechless. *I know Peter would go in a heartbeat, but how? I have the other kids and Thomas or wait, I don't have the other kids. . . The other kids are all leaving this week. I just have Shiloh and Peter. I don't have anything here I need to do. Thomas is off having an amazing summer, and he never asked me.*

"Anne, are you still here?"

"How would it work? Would I drive?" Anne had so many questions.

"Well, I have a bus and a driver because I can't drive. I get tired. I do have some crew who travel in another bus with us. We stay in hotels when we get to the cities on the tour, but my bus is comfortable and big enough for all of us. You can ride with me so, it won't cost you anything."

Anne was immediately disappointed as she realized she could never afford to stay in hotels on their budget this summer. "Are you still there?" Exa asked again.

"I am. It's really a tremendous offer, and so generous, but Thomas isn't working all summer. I don't think I can afford to be on the road with two kids even if we ride with you." Anne's heart sank a little lower with each word as she declined the offer.

"My mistake, I wasn't clear, the tour pays for the hotels; it's all figured in. I'll just have my manager add a room for you guys. I would also like to compensate Pe ta for his time."

"Compensate?"

"Yes, I get paid to play, so if Pe ta plays, I will make sure he gets a percentage. It will be a smaller amount, miniscule really, but it would be something. I wouldn't treat him any differently than any other professional, opening artist. My manager can figure out the details and get your contract."

You want to pay Peter to do something he loves, plus take him on vacation. Anne heart was starting to flutter in excitement, but she needed to make sure she wasn't missing anything. "How long are you going to be touring?"

"My tour lasts seventeen weeks, but I was thinking you could just come for the first leg of it; it starts in Minneapolis. Then on June 23, I play in Chicago. I thought maybe you could fly back after that one unless you want to stay longer. So, maybe you could come with me for a little over three weeks?"

"Let me get this straight . . . you want Peter, Shiloh, and me to come on your bus and go on tour with you? It's all paid for, and Peter will even get a paycheck for playing?" Anne was giddy as she repeated the details. *I think Peter would be comfortable riding on a bus even with his braces. His legs shouldn't get cramped. I can make food and bring it along. Shiloh rides easy in a car seat; bless his heart, he's the best baby.* Her mind flew through the "mom" details she needed to address.

"Yeah, how does that sound?"

"It sounds fantastic! I know Peter will die when he finds out. He loves playing in front of people. When do we leave?" *I can't believe I just said, "Yes". I'm going on tour with a rock star! Me, Anne Arnold, mother of five. Well, not a rock star, but a music celebrity.*

"Two days. We leave the day after tomorrow at 7 a.m. Can you be ready?"

"That's perfect. We'll be there," Anne agreed.

Eighteen

Anne pushed her daydream out of her head as she rushed back to the hospital to return to Peter. Her phone rang as she parked the van. The caller I.D. told her it was Sammy, Peter's manager. She was immediately embarrassed that she had never thought to give him an update on Peter's health, Anne said, "Hello."

"'Anne. It's Sammy."

"Hi, how are you?"

"I'm fine. How's Peter?"

"I feel bad I didn't call you. It's been crazy, but yeah, I think he should wake up later today . . . at least that's what his doctor said," Anne rambled as she searched the floor boards under the passenger seat for her purse.

"That's good news. Please let me know if I can do anything," Sammy offered. "I don't want to be in the way, but I can help with anything you need."

"That's sweet of you to offer. I'll let you know, but right now, we're just waiting."

"I hope you don't think it's rude for me to give you an update on Peter's tour right now, but just so you know things are taken care of, I did go ahead and cancel the rest of the tour – officially. I had all the tickets refunded."

Anne let out an involuntary sigh. *It seemed so final. It took Peter nine months to get ready for this tour and all that effort meant nothing right now.*

Sammy added, "I would like to reschedule the tour later, if Peter wishes, but I wanted all his business affairs to be wrapped up at this point."

"Of course. It makes sense. Thank you for handling that."

"It's no problem. But, I suppose I'll let you get back to Peter. Please be in touch."

"I will. Thanks Sammy. Goodbye." Anne ended the call. She yanked hard on her purse as she tried to retrieve it from where it had rolled under the passenger seat, but it was stuck on something. She pulled harder, and the strap gave way. It was free now, but the strap was broken, hanging loose on one end. In a moment of overwhelm, she screamed as hard as she could. It wasn't so much the strap, but more the thought of Peter's hard work going to waste. *Peter put everything into his work and it was all gone!*

This was the first year in twelve years Anne and Peter would not be hitting the road to tour. The tour cancellation solidified Peter's condition to Anne, who was trying to live in denial. Things really had changed drastically. *What I wouldn't give to go back and do it all again.* Those early days on tour were magical.

* * *

Anne remembered standing in front of Exa's house with a suitcase in one hand and Shiloh on her opposite hip. Peter's mouth dropped when he saw the big, white, tour bus. "We're riding in that," he pointed his finger at it.

"I think so," Anne said as her nervous tummy churned. She had anxiety to be away from her kids, she was uneasy for the overseas flight Marie and Thomas were currently on, and she was nervous over this tour.

"Over here!" Exa leaned out on one leg from the bus door. "Set your bags on the sidewalk and my driver, Rick, will put them below." Exa smiled – a rare facial expression for her.

"I can't believe we're doing this," Anne said as she carried Shiloh onto the bus. Peter led the way.

"This is amazing! It has a TV and a kitchen. Mom look, it has a bathroom!" Peter walked all over the bus. "Were do I get to sit?" Peter asked Exa.

"You can sit wherever you like. I have blankets and pillows in this cabinet. The fridge is stocked with drinks and snacks; help yourself. It's pretty comfortable riding." Exa pulled out a grey fleece blanket, she wrapped it around herself, and sat in a recliner next to the door.

"It's very nice," Anne said as she folded one leg under her to sit on the sofa next to Peter. Anne held Shiloh in her lap. He chewed on a teething ring while Anne tried to keep him from drooling over all her. Rick finished loading the luggage, and was sitting at the steering wheel waiting to drive.

"Well Pe ta, are you ready for your first tour?" Exa asked.

"Yes, let's tour!" Peter yelled and stuck both his fists in the air. He giggled, and then was quiet for a second. He looked to his mom, he whispered, "Can I use the bathroom?"

"Yes, honey, you can use it. Exa said make yourself at home."

"Good, I'm really glad we have our own bathroom."

"Me too," Anne agreed.

Exa smirked, and then hunched over a book, looking like she wanted to be quiet. They settled into a groove quickly, and traveled well together. Peter constantly gazed out the window, and Anne tried to keep Shiloh from chewing on everything.

A few hours later, Peter did a walk through at the auditorium. "Mom, look at the size of this room!"

Anne's stomach dropped. "It's huge. Exa said this show's sold out too. All these seats are going to be filled in a few hours. Are you ready?"

"Yeah, I know I can do it." Peter's eyes continued to survey the room.

"You're my hero then because this is a pretty big deal."

"Hey mom, I was thinking. . ."

"What baby?" Anne said as she adjusted Shiloh in his baby sling on her chest. He had started to fuss because he was trying to get down.

"I need a stage name."

"What?" Anne looked up.

"You know how Exa made up her name so people don't know her real name."

"Yeah, a stage name is actually a good idea. Do you know what you want to be called?"

"I was thinking about it in the bus. It should sound special. I think I would get confused if I had a different first name. Like, if I said my name was Frank and people called me Frank, I would forget to answer them."

Anne nodded. "That would be tough. You could probably keep the same first name. Peter's a great name."

Peter nodded his head, "I'm keeping my first name. My stage name's going to be Peter Ruby."

Anne furrowed her eyebrows. "How did you come up with that?"

"Do you remember when you told me that I was the ruby in the water of rocks?"

Anne nodded her head. Peter continued, "I really do think I'm the ruby."

"Me too," Anne agreed wholeheartedly, "I don't think I could think of a better name for you."

"Good, it's settled."

"Do you think we should let Exa know so she knows to call you that tonight?" Anne asked.

"Yeah, and you need to call me that, too." Peter playfully pointed his finger at Anne. Then he added, "I don't need anyone overhearing my real name."

"Well, okay then Mr. Ruby." Anne smiled. "Exa went back to her dressing room. She said you have a little room back here, too." Anne pointed to a doorway behind the stage. They walked backstage and down the hall.

"Mom, there's my name in the star on the door! It says Peter. Good thing they never used Arnold," Peter whispered the last part to Anne.

"Hey you two," Exa called from across the hall. "I thought I heard you. Are you getting excited?"

"Exa, guess what?" Peter ran to her.

"What?"

"I have a stage name. You can't call me Peter Arnold any more. Call me Peter Ruby."

"Peter Ruby. Rubies are precious gemstones. I like that," Exa said "Did you find your tux?"

"Huh?"

"Wardrobe put a tux in your room. Try it on now to make sure it fits. There's still enough time before the show, if some alterations need to be made, but we need to know now." Peter started to run back to his door to find his tux. "Wait, Peter," Exa called. Peter stopped and spun on his heels to look back at her. "I'm going to go down for my sound check here in a few minutes. You can come up in about half an hour to do your sound check."

Peter nodded, turned around, twisted the doorknob to his dressing room, and flung his door wide opened. "Mom, Look!" Peter pointed to a table loaded with an enormous sandwich platter and a tray of brownies. "Is that for me?"

"It's in your room so I would say so," Anne said. "Don't eat all the brownies though. We can take them with us."

"We can take all of it with us. I can't eat or drink anything before I play," Peter said as he turned away from the spread and walked back to the sitting area.

"Why not?"

Peter glared at his mom, "You know what happened last time."

"Yeah, I remember, but you don't play for at least three hours. You can have a sandwich now."

Peter thought for a moment, and then agreed, "Okay, I can have one, but I'm cutting myself off once I go to sound check." Peter walked back to the table and selectively picked out a brownie with no crust.

"Peter, look at this tux. It has tails." Anne held up his suit.

"Huh?" Peter turned his head.

"See how the jacket's long in the back. I have to get a picture of you in this." Anne flipped the tails for movement. "It's so cute! Go try it on."

The tux fit perfectly, the sandwiches were excellent, and sound check went well. It was time for Peter to get dressed. "Let me put some gel in your hair and comb it back off your face," Anne said as she pulled hair product from her bag.

"Huh?"

"Yeah, it'll make you look professional." She squeezed a glob into her palm, and then applied it to his hair, pulling it through the ends of his hair with her fingers.

"It feels sort of crunchy." Peter patted the top of his head.

"Yeah it does. It gives you a new look for Mr. Ruby."

They were interrupted by a knocking on Peter's dressing room.

"Hey, I'm Carrie, Exa's manager. We spoke on the phone." She held out her hand.

"Yes, good to put a face to your name." Anne took her hand and shook it. "This is Mr. Ruby," Anne said to Carrie.

"Nice to meet you, Mr. Ruby." She smiled at Peter. "I just got done speaking with Exa about your performance, and I think we're going to have you go on right after intermission. I know she originally thought you should go on before the show, but she has another opening artist for this part of the tour. If you went before the opening act, no one will even be seated, because it'll be too early. If we wait until after intermission, everyone will be seated, so you'll get a better audience."

Peter looked at Carrie. She was tall for a girl. She had to be well over six-feet tall with soft facial features and light blond hair swept back into a low, professional bun.

"How does that sound?" She bent down to Peter's eye level.

"It sounds good." Peter swallowed hard.

"Great," she said. "It is nice to meet you both . . ., well three of you." She glanced at sleeping Shiloh in the corner. "You'll see a lot of me on this tour. If you need anything, don't hesitate to ask."

"Thank you so much for having us and for your help," Anne said.

"My pleasure. We're excited to have Peter on the tour. I can't wait to hear him play. See you in a bit," She said as she closed the door.

Peter, Anne, and Shiloh sat on the couch in the dressing room, watching Exa's play on the TV. "This is cool, mom." Peter beamed as his eyes held on to every move Exa made.

"Yep, that's going to be you in about forty-five minutes. Are you ready?" Anne elbowed him.

"I can't wait."

Exa was striking; she possessed a stage presence Anne had never seen before. For a moment, Anne's mind wondered back to that nagging question about Exa's intentions with helping Peter. *Ah, don't think too much about it. Just live in the moment,* she told herself.

"Oh man, mom, she's bowing. Exa stood up! People are clapping; she's done. It's intermission. Mom, it's time. I have to go to the bathroom! I have to go right now. Do I have time?" Peter's words raced as fast as his mind. His cheeks flushed red.

"Yes, Peter. Go to the bathroom and relax. You are the show. It can't go on without you." Anne tried to appear composed. The butterflies in her stomach were like walruses flopping around in her tummy. *I know he'll play well, but I hope it ends well, too.*

A knock sounded from the door. "That's Carrie. You go to the bathroom. I'll grab your jacket and let her in." Anne ran to the door.

"Hey, Carrie, I'm so nervous." Anne whispered under her breath.

"It's a lot to take in," Carrie said with a pleasant smile as she leaned against the door frame. "We're slightly behind schedule, so we need to be out there now."

"Sure, Peter had to use the restroom first. He'll be one minute. We both are so appreciative to Exa for this opportunity. It's just amazing," Anne said nervously as she stared at the closed bathroom door, waiting for Peter.

"Yeah, Exa has never taken anyone on tour with her before. I about fell off my chair when she told me she wanted to bring someone, let alone an undiscovered kid."

"Really? I had no idea. When she invited us, she made it sound like she always has guest artists," Anne said.

"She has opening artists, but they don't travel together. She needs her space, and she can be a talent snob. So, I'm curious to hear Peter play." Anne's stomach tightened with Carrie's words.

"I'm ready." Peter ran to the door.

"Here, I'll hold your jacket while you put your arms in here. You need this ear piece on, too," Anne said as she assisted Peter. Then, Carrie ushered them both down the hall.

Exa stood at the stage door, drinking a bottle of water. "Phew, those lights are warm tonight." She fanned herself as they approached. "Are you ready?" She looked at Peter.

"Yeah."

"Stand by this door until I announce your name. This is it, Pe ta. This is my cue. See you in a bit." Exa waved as she walked out onto the stage, and the audience erupted in applause.

Peter turned to his mom without smiling as he was all professional, but Anne could see a sparkle in his eye. *Man, do I love this little boy. If only I could bottle this moment.* "I love you, Peter. Don't worry about playing; just have fun." Anne hugged him.

"I love you too, mom."

Through the door, they could hear Exa speaking, "It's so great to be here. Let's give a hand to my band! They've been with me through the last five tours. I'm ecstatic to have them back." The audience clapped loudly. "Thank you all for coming out tonight. I have the best audiences." She paused to wait for their applause. She continued, "I have a surprise addition to my program. Let me introduce you to a friend I've made this last year. You'll see for yourself how special he is. His name is Pe Ta Ruby, and he's five years old. He's here to play his original piece, "The Goat Woman". Without further ado, help me welcome Mr. Ruby!"

Carrie nodded for Peter to go on stage, Anne winked at him, and he walked onto the stage.

Nineteen

PETER

Anne didn't waste time waiting for the slow hospital elevators. She darted up the stairs two at a time, and arrived in Peter's room out of breath. She glanced at Thomas, who was reading a medical journal in the chair at Peter's bedside. "How is he?" Anne asked as she walked to the wooden rocking chair in the corner of the room.

"Good. They adjusted his medicine again. He should wake up soon. How are you?" Thomas asked as he crossed his leg toward Anne.

"I just want to talk to Peter." Anne sat down and set her purse under the chair.

"What about?" Thomas stretched his arms behind his head as if he was moving for the first time in a while.

"Anything really. I miss his voice." Anne's eyes fell to the floor and her dangling purse strap that stuck out like a tail from under the chair. "Oh, Sammy called and said he would love to help in any way he can."

"That's nice. Is that all he called for?"

". . . and to tell us that he officially cancelled the tour. We knew that though. . ."

"I don't think we'll be worrying about concerts for a while."

"I was sad when I realized how much Peter's immediate future had changed."

"You're just now realizing that?" Thomas closed the medical journal, and leaned over to Anne, touching her arm.

"I think so. You know me. I like to hide inside my head instead of face reality." Anne sighed as she closed her eyes in thought.

"You do what you need to do to get through this." Thomas retrieved his arm and leaned back in his chair. "You always preferred to rip the Band-Aid off a little slower than most people."

"I do like to spread it out as much as I can," Anne agreed. "What I wouldn't do to be able to be on tour with Peter right now. I was remembering that first tour. I was so proud of him. He walked out on stage like an old pro."

"I wish I could've been there."

"I will never forget it."

Peter drifted in a lighter sleep as his meds started to wear off. He heard his parents talk about his tour being cancelled; that stung. *All my hard work . . . gone.* Like his mother, he preferred to live in his head, over facing reality. To avoid thinking of his canceled tour, he reminisced about his first tour concert, too. It was a moment, no, it was THE moment that changed his life forever.

＊ ＊ ＊

He was only five-years-old the first time he played professionally but a part of him knew that he was exactly where he was supposed to be. Normally, he was used to his leg braces, but that night, he felt like they added ten pounds to each leg. He took small steps to conceal them as well as his awkward stride. He caught Exa's eye as he rounded the corner which gave him the boost he needed.

He rubbed his finger joints one last time. The audience clapped until Peter sat at the piano. He didn't want to look at them. There were so many of them – way more than he pictured when the room was empty. The lights overhead dimmed and the crowd hushed. A white spotlight warmed Peter's face, comforting him like July sunshine.

Peter imagined the spotlight was the sun, and he was outside all alone. He took one last deep, cleansing breath out and lightly pressed the first keys. Fearlessly, Peter preformed his piece, "The Goat Woman" like he had a message to get out to everyone. He needed people to hear his thoughts. *This woman watches me while I sleep. I see her outside my window at night. I know it's her, but no one will tell me why.* They were all strangers, but for one, brief moment, Peter had their attention and made sure nothing stole his time with them.

As swiftly as the moment arrived, it faded. Peter took his hand from the last key. Roaring applause filled the auditorium. Peter looked up to see the audience. People were on their feet as they cheered. Peter stood up, memorized at their enthusiasm and he drank it all in. A voice came over his earpiece, telling him to bow. *Oh Yes! The bowing is my favorite part.* He stepped away from his bench, faced the crowd, and gave a deep bow. Out of the corner of his eye, he saw a figure walking towards him; it was Exa.

She grabbed his hand and pulled him down in another bow. She smiled. It was so rare to see that women smile that Peter had to look twice. She actually looked joyous. Exa grabbed the microphone and, over the noise, she said, "Ladies and gentleman, Pe Ta Ruby – just five years old!" The crowd roared some more. *I had no idea people could make this much noise.* He fought the instinct to cover his ears. The energy was explosive.

Exa leaned in and hugged Peter. "You were brilliant Pe Ta. Now go meet your mom backstage; she's dying to hug you," she whispered in his ear.

Peter floated back off the stage as people continued to cheer. "Peter, you were amazing! They loved you." Anne tackled him with a hug and kisses. "How do you feel?"

"I feel good. I think they liked it."

"Did you hear the applause? They loved it!"

Peter giggled, "Can we go back to my room now? I could really use a brownie."

"Anything you want. Tonight is your night," Anne said.

Twenty

ANNE

The morning after five-year-old Peter's first concert, the group was back on the bus heading for their next town and another concert. "Peter, Dad's on the phone." Anne put her phone on speaker so they could all hear and then gave it to him.

"Hello," Peter said.

"Hey there bud. Congrats on the big night. You looked awesome," Thomas said.

"You were there?" Peter asked.

"No, I saw it on the Internet."

"It's on the Internet?" Peter looked to his mom inquisitively.

"How did that happen?" Anne asked Exa.

"Ah, people always take videos. They aren't supposed to, but it always happens. Here, I can look on my computer." Exa started searching.

"Yeah, you looked great. How do you feel?" Thomas continued.

"I feel good. I had fun. Dad, they gave me a whole huge plate of sandwiches and brownies all to myself; it was so much food," Peter said.

"That's great. I bet it was fun. I'm so proud of you. Well, I hate to cut this short, but I should get going. I don't want to miss my ride home, but I just wanted to say I saw you. I'm sorry I missed it, but I love you so much. I'll have Marie call tonight."

"Okay, Dad."

"Bye."

"Bye," Peter said as he ended the call. "Mom, Dad says I'm on the Internet!"

"Here it is, Pe Ta. I found it." Exa held up her laptop. "Someone uploaded this; look at the comments. Everyone's talking about how talented you are. There's over 90,000 hits already."

"I can't believe I'm on the Internet," Peter said as he leaned over to see Exa's computer.

Anne was silent. *It never dawned on me before, but Peter's fully exposed. I had no idea something like this would happen – after only one show.* "Is it good that it's on the Internet like that?" Anne looked at Exa.

"Any exposure for the tour is good, and all the comments are saying how great he is. It's a good thing. I don't pay attention to the reviews myself. I used to follow them, but I learned to do the best I can and be happy with that."

Anne looked at Peter, "We're here to have fun. We aren't going to care about that stuff either." She took Exa's computer away from Peter and returned it to Exa.

Peter sighed, "Can I call Tane and Paul?"

"We do need to touch base with them. Great idea." Anne called the cabin from her phone. Grandpa answered, and he too, had already looked up Peter's video online.

The Internet buzzed with what little information people knew about Peter Ruby. As the tour went on, more videos popped up. People tried to steal photographs of him. It wasn't long before people started calling Exa's manager to see if they could get more information about Peter. Anne declined all contact with the media. She didn't want to expose Peter to anything like that.

Denying the media access to Peter only had the opposite effect; it made people more aggressive, wanting to know who the mysterious piano prodigy was and how he ended up on tour with Exa. Exa always introduced him as a friend she had met this last year and never offered any more introduction or information. Unamused by all the attention, Exa ignored it.

Anne's paranoia with the media came to a head one morning when she ran into a gas station while the bus was filling up. She grabbed some batteries and some snacks. She, with Shiloh in his sling, waited near the counter to pay for her items. Her eyes wondered over to the magazines until she caught sight of something that stunned her. Afraid to avert her eye, as if someone could read her thoughts, she froze.

"Ma'am. It's your turn," the lady behind the counter called to her. Anne fumbled as she moved toward the rack, staring at and reaching for it — a tabloid with the headlines: *"Identity Revealed: 5-Year-old Peter Ruby's a forty-year-old midget!"* Below the headline was a bad photo of Exa. Some captions explained how Exa was dating this "little person" and to bring attention to the tour, she brought him along. Anne flipped to the article that went on to say the reason Peter Ruby doesn't want to talk to the media is because people would learn he is a grown man!

Quickly, Anne closed the magazine, trying to push the image out of her mind. She paid for her stuff, rushed back to the bus, which was ready to depart. Anne needed time to think. *I try so hard to be a good parent; I had no idea something like this would happen. All I wanted to do was have a little fun with Peter this summer and give him a chance to build his self-esteem.*

Relieved there was only one more show, Anne needed a fresh perspective so she whispered to Exa when Peter was busy with a video, "Psst. Exa." Anne nodded her head for Exa to follow her into the back bedroom of the bus.

"I need to talk to you," Anne said, once the door was shut.

"Yeah, what about?" Exa plopped down on the bed and folded her legs crisscross style. Her black hair was parted in the middle and the ends dangled low, brushing the tops of her legs. In that moment, Exa appeared childlike to Anne. Anne realized she had spent the last year of her life hanging out with this woman and she knew practically nothing about her. She didn't even know her age. "Anne, what's up?" Exa leaned forward.

Anne cleared her throat. "I saw something when I was in that gas station." Anne sat on the corner of the bed to talk softly, so Peter wouldn't hear. "It was tabloid magazine, and you were on the cover. It said they found Peter's identity, and he was really a forty-year-old man who was really short and that you two were dating."

"Ha! Oh my, that's a good one." Exa snorted as she laughed. "They come up with the craziest stuff."

"That doesn't bother you?"

"No! No one believes that stuff. It's all bread and circuses. You should see all the headlines I have read about me over the years."

"But, it's a lie," Anne defended her position of hurt.

"Yeah, but it *sells* and makes money. That's what they do . . .," Exa's voice trailed off as she saw Anne's face was flushed and the lines on her forehead wrinkled. "Look Anne, it comes with the territory. Let it roll off your back. It certainly won't be the last thing they print."

"Peter's just a child. Is there nothing sacred?" Anne asked.

"Not when it comes to selling stories."

Anne looked at the wall. "I'm regretting coming on this tour. I didn't want this to happen; I didn't know it could."

"Nothing happened. Look at Peter. He's alive and *loving* this experience. He's blossomed on this tour. Would you want to take that away from him? You can go back home, and no one will even know about him back in Minnesota because no one knows it was him. You told everyone you were going to the cabin with the boys in Montana. Who would suspect it would be Peter back there? He doesn't even go to school. After you get home, everything will die down. All you will have left of this tour will be the great memories of seeing Peter happy. Trust me. The tabloids will move on and find someone else to pick on."

Exa was very convincing. *No one would know who Peter really was, and he was having fun. Still . . .* Anne was even more relieved there was only one last show before they would part ways.

They arrived in Chicago later that day; both Peter and Anne were glued to the window. Buildings blanketed the skyline as far as they could see. Chicago was going to be the last stop for Peter and Anne, but it was also special because Grandpa was planning to surprise Peter by bringing Paul and Tane up to see the show.

This show was a big deal for Exa too. "Chicago's a big blues city," she explained. "The music scene's an extremely important part of the culture, and I really need good reviews here to help record sales."

"You look worried," Anne said.

"I just hate Chicago."

"Why? You said they love music here."

"Yeah, they do. I have a history with this city. When I first started in the biz, I uh, I really lost part of my soul here. . ." Exa looked blankly out the window.

Not wanting to pry, Anne changed the subject. She stretched her hands above her head and yawned. "I'm glad we have the night off. I can't wait to try some pizza. I think we're going to relax at the hotel tonight. I saw online that they have a great pool. I was thinking maybe tomorrow we could get up early to hit the zoo before sound check. Do you think we would have time for the zoo tomorrow?"

Exa never answered Anne as she continued to stare out the window. Anne retracted her attention and focused on Shiloh, who was trying to chew on her necklace. *Something's bothering Exa, but it's not my place to press the issue. I'm glad this is the last show.* Grateful as ever for the pleasant moments, Anne was getting uncomfortable with some of the caveats, and she could tell Exa needed her own space back.

Looking up suddenly with focus, Exa stood and walked back toward her private room, "I'm going to call Ambrose," she said.

"Who?" Just as Anne looked up, Shiloh threw up on her sleeve.

"Ambrose, My husband." Exa closed the door cutting off the conversation.

Anne dabbed at the spot of vomit on her sleeve with a wipe, but it wasn't coming clean. When she looked up to ask Exa another question, she saw the closed door. "Here, Peter, hold your brother. I need to change my shirt." Peter took Shiloh. Anne changed her shirt and then ran her dirty sleeve under water at the kitchen sink. *I think this is only the second time Exa has mentioned her husband and I have known her for months.* Anne realized how mysterious Exa was as she didn't share many layers of her personal life with anyone. She could understand the need for privacy after the morning she had with the tabloids. Exa's secrecy started to make sense to Anne, and she not only understood it, but appreciated it. *Maybe secrecy was the key to being in the business as long as Exa had been because you never know who you can trust.*

Twenty-one

A light tapping resonated from Peter's hospital-room doorway. Anne was expecting to see the doctor but instead, she was surprised to see a young lady leaning against the door frame, holding a bouquet of purple lilies. She had soft blond curls cut short to frame her face and large, shining blue eyes. Anne immediately recognized her and welcomed her, "Gwen! Come here, let me hug you. It's great to see you."

Anne embraced Gwen. Then, Gwen turned to Thomas, "Hi Thomas, how are you?"

"I'm doing alright. It's great to see you," he said.

"How is he?" Gwen asked as she walked over to Peter's bedside.

"We expect him to wake up at any moment," Anne said.

"That's great," Gwen looked at her friend. "It seems so weird for the roles to be reversed."

Anne slowly nodded in agreement. *It is quite the role reversal. Gwen's usually the ill one and that was precisely the reason why Peter and she even met all those years ago.*

. . .

Anne remembered the day she met Gwen. It had been the last day of Peter's first tour. Anne had just gotten Shiloh up from his nap. She noticed she had a missed call on her cell phone. She listened to the message and rolled her eyes when she heard it was from Exa's manager. Again. Gritting her teeth, she dialed Carrie's number.

"Hey, did you call?"

"Yes, Anne, I know you already made it clear this morning you don't want Peter to talk with anyone, but I got a call from someone who wants to meet Peter."

Anne sighed. "What? No, I already said this is the last day of the tour. We go home tomorrow. We're not doing that."

"Anne, it was Make-a-Wish."

"Huh?"

"A counselor from Make-a-Wish called me. Do you know the charity that grants wishes to kids who are terminally ill?"

"Yeah, I know who they are. My husband's a doctor. What did they want?"

"There's a little girl here in the city who has been following the tour online. She went to the first show in Minneapolis, but now she's in Chicago visiting her grandmother. She wanted to go to the show tonight, but the tickets have been sold out for a while."

"She wants tickets?"

"Well, yeah, and she used her Make-a-Wish opportunity for the tickets so her counselor thought it would be neat to get a backstage pass for her to meet Peter. Do you think that would be okay?"

"I can ask him." Anne placed her hand over the phone and turned towards Peter. "Honey, there's a little girl who wants to meet you tonight. She's sick and a charity called Make-a-Wish wants to grant her wish which is to come see the show and meet you."

"Why does she want to meet me?" Peter asked.

"I guess she saw you play in Minnesota and she must've really liked it. Would you feel comfortable if she came backstage before the show to say 'hi' for a moment?"

"Yeah, that's fine."

Anne held the phone back up to her ear, "He said that's fine. Will you let me know about what time when you find out?"

"Sure, that works for me. I'll see you later," Carrie replied. Anne hung up the phone and turned to Peter, who looked worried.

"Mom, she's going to be nice to me, right?" Peter asked.

"Yeah honey, she wants to meet you because she admires you. Of course, she'll be nice to you."

"Okay, just checking because most kids are mean to me," Peter stated so plainly, Anne was waiting for Peter to give a punchline, but it never came. He wasn't joking. *Poor kid. Peter has no friends his age. Exa's probably his only non-family-related contact and she definitely isn't his peer. I guess maybe this tour wasn't such a bad idea after all. It does give him a positive hobby to focus on.*

A few hours later, Anne, Peter, and Shiloh were resting backstage when there was a knock at the door that interrupted their preshow, traditional go–fish game. "I'll see who it is," Anne said as she darted to the door, still holding her cards in her hand. She cracked the door open and stuck her nose out. A smile busted over her face as she flung open the door and grabbed both Tane and Paul in a bear hug. Grandpa stood behind them. He looked both tired and relieved.

"Come in," Anne said.

"Mom, who is it?" Peter pivoted to look toward the door. "Paul! Tane! Grandpa! Did you come to see my show?"

"We sure did! We couldn't miss it," Grandpa said as he scooped Peter up in a hug.

"Awesome! I'm so excited. Hey, do you want a sandwich? I get a whole tray. Here look." Peter's brothers, who had gigantic appetites typical of growing boys, walked over to the tray, and were both impressed by all the food. The boys reunited with stories of their travels over the sandwiches.

"Are you worn out?" Anne asked Grandpa as she led him to the sofa. He sat his pudgy body on the end of the coach, leaning all the way back and putting one foot on the coffee table in front of him. His brown eyes glistened as he took off his glasses to wipe them with the end of his blue, flannel shirt.

"No, not too bad, but I'll be glad to get my regular afternoon naps in again. We had fun." He chuckled, then set his glasses back on his nose. "How are you holding up?"

"We're great. It seems like it has been much longer than three weeks. So much has happened. I've been a little stressed about all the attention Peter has been getting in the media."

"You go on tour with a world-famous musician and you're surprised the media's snooping around, taking notice." Grandpa laughed from deep in his chest.

"Yeah, I guess I learned my lesson the hard way." Another knock came from the door. "Oh, that must be our guest," Anne said as she hurried to the door, opening it to see Carrie with two other ladies and a little girl.

Carrie spoke, "Hi Anne, this is Amanda from Make-a-Wish and she is here with Gwenevere and her mom, Olivia."

"Hi, we've been expecting you. Come on in." Anne opened the door wider. The little girl looked to be about Peter's age. She wore a scarf around her head concealing, yet displaying at the same time, the fact that she had no hair. Pale and skinny, with dark circles under her eyes, she didn't hold back on her big personality as she walked into the room, scoping it out.

Gwenevere's mother wore the child's illness in the lines on her face. Anne took one look at the women and her heart felt compassion. She knew all too well the exhausting task of taking care of a sick child.

"Peter," Anne said, "Your guests are here."

Peter looked up from his sandwich tray. He finished chewing while he walked over to them. He stopped at the fridge to grab a bouquet of purple lilies Carrie had bought for him to give to Gwenevere as a gift.

"Hi Gwenevere, I got you roses," Peter stumbled over the last syllable in her name as he held out the flowers.

Her eyes popped wide open, "Thank you. You can call me Gwen."

"Gwen," Peter repeated.

"I think these are lilies," Gwen said as she looked at her bouquet.

"Oh, sorry. I guess I got you lilies."

"That's okay. They're pretty. I can't wait to see you play the piano again. I saw you before in Minneapolis and I never saw anything like it. When did you learn to play?" Gwen asked.

"I just taught myself this last year. I had music class at school and my teacher let me play her piano. I had to quit school later, but then I met Exa, and she let me play her piano too."

"Oh, I don't go to school either. I used to, but my mom said the kids might get me sick. I have a tutor now. It's nice because she lets me wear my pajamas when I work."

"I wear my pajamas too when I do my school work! That's the best part." Peter's face lite up as he realized they had something in common. "Being at home for school is better. Don't ya think?"

"Sometimes. But, I sometimes get bored." Gwen smiled slyly. "Then I miss it. But mostly, I miss my friends."

"Oh, I don't get bored because I play piano. I don't miss my friends because I didn't have any," Peter said frankly. "Hey, I have an idea, you can call me when you're bored at home because I'm at home too!"

Gwen's smiled broadened. "Yeah, that's an awesome idea."

Olivia placed her hand on Gwen's shoulder and softly interrupted, "I think we need to be going. Peter needs to get ready for his show. Can you say, 'Thank you'?"

Gwen obliged her mother. After the door closed behind them, Peter watched the emptiness of the doorway for a moment before asking, "Was her hair gone because she's sick?"

"I think so," Anne said. She was suddenly relieved Peter didn't ask his question in front of Gwen. Paul and Tane started talking and the room was instantly noisy again. Soon, it was show time for Peter. The family had front row seats in the audience; even Anne was going to sit with them to see what it looked like from the audience. *This was it. This was the last show – thank goodness.*

In the audience, Anne held Shiloh in her seat, nestled between Tane and Paul, and Grandpa was on the end. Peter looked professional and happy as he played. *He has grown the last couple weeks. He pays more attention to the audience and smiles a lot more.* When Peter was done, she enthusiastically applauded, never feeling more proud, as Peter bowed and left the stage.

The family stayed in their seats to watch Exa finished her segment. After a few minutes of steady applause, Exa returned with Peter to play their new encore – an original song, "Lightening and Rainbows". Lively and a bit jazzy, the song was one of their favorite ones that they made up somewhere between Sioux Falls and Chicago. They were playing it tonight as a special encore addition since it was their final performance.

The audience responded well to the song and the pair did a double bow, then headed off the stage one last time. Anne couldn't get out of her chair as she was instantly trapped by people squeezing toward the door; she decided to wait until the crowd thinned out to leave, but Peter beat them by coming out to meet them.

"Mom, what did you think of "Lightening and Rainbows"?" Peter asked as he walked up next to his family. He had removed his jacket and put on a t-shirt to blend in.

"I loved it," Anne said. Peter was proud to hear his big brothers congratulate him. He was always in their shadows, so it felt great to be admired. The stadium was now empty as they shared in jovial conversation. Sighing in a silent moment, Anne said, "We need to head back to your dressing room. Exa arranged a surprise, send-off party for you – with cake," she winked.

The family headed backstage, except for Peter, who grabbed his mom's arm and whispered, "Can I go on stage by myself one last time? I want to look around, so I can remember it always."

"Sure. We'll be in your room when you're ready." Anne touched the top of his head to smooth his hair, then left him by himself.

Peter climbed the stairs to the stage. He noticed some of the maintenance people had already begun to clean up. He ran his fingers along the top of the piano keys, then glanced up to notice the way the empty seats looked back at him. Peter knew this tour was ending, but he needed to feel the butterflies one more time. Closing his eyes, he imagined the people standing on their feet and cheering.

For Peter, this was a tremendous, life-changing experience that would forever set his life on a different path. Though, unaware of his upcoming journey at the time, he thought the butterflies were over. Saying goodbye to the feeling, goodbye to the butterflies, he bowed one last time.

He raised his body up and stood. Startled, he saw he was not alone. His eyes focused on the figure standing dead center two rows in, only about fifteen feet from Peter: his eyes locked hers and he froze. Ice ran through his veins and fear knotted his stomach as he identified the ghostly green eyes that had been forever burned in his brain; the Goat Woman!

She was standing right there in front of him. Peter's voice stuck in his throat. *She knows my song's about her! She heard my Goat Woman song, and she wants to get revenge!*

Adrenaline surged through his veins, and he scurried offstage, running straight to his room, where his family was gathered in celebration. He gravitated toward his mom who he looked to for comfort and protection as he concentrated on blending in because the Goat Woman's presence had alarmed him. When the party was over, he was ready to go. He thanked Exa, but he remained mute about the night's events. He was glad the tour was over; it was time to go home.

That summer had set up a tradition for the Arnold family. Peter continued to be homeschooled and to work with Exa during the school year. Each summer, she invited him back on her tour for the first two weeks. Years passed, Peter's fan base grew, and as it blossomed, Anne became a little more comfortable with the exposure – even allowing him to get a fan website. Time rushed by like the beating of a drum, and in what seemed like a blink of an eye, the Arnold's found themselves saying goodbye to Peter as he had graduated from homeschool at the age of 17, already a world-renowned pianist.

Twenty-Two

"So, what brings you to town?" Anne asked Gwen as she blinked away her memories, focusing on the present moment. Peter's hospital room was seeped in a heavy silence with Gwen guarding Peter's side.

"I just drove up for the day to see Peter," Gwen said as she tucked a curl behind her ear.

"That's sweet of you," Anne said. "Have you talked to him lately?"

"I called him right before the show to wish him luck and to ask about my backstage pass. It was weird though. He sounded upset or something. Do you think he wasn't feeling well?"

Peter could hear Gwen's voice as he was sleeping lighter than normally. He knew exactly what he was upset about two days ago — Exa Scarletta. He tried to squeeze Gwen's hand to respond to her presence, but he failed because he couldn't move his hands. He wanted desperately to tell Gwen what had happened.

* * *

It was just two days ago, and Peter had been busy packing for his tour while he kept his phone glued to his ear, talking to his manager, Sammy. He flew through the kitchen to grab something to eat because he was in hurry but his stomach wouldn't stop growling. "Got a minute?" Anne asked from where she was standing by the kitchen sink.

"Depends." Peter ravenously attacked his cold-cut sandwich with a vengeance.

"I know you're busy, but there's something you might want to see in the garage." Anne pointed out the window to the garage.

Confused, and knowing he really didn't have time for games, he shrugged his shoulders and sighed, "I guess, it'd better be fast. Did you get me a new car for graduation?" He grinned and bit into his sandwich; mayo dripped out of the corner of his mouth. He shoved another bit of his sandwich into his mouth until his cheeks puffed out, and he could barely close his mouth to chew. Holding his sandwich, he walked out the backdoor towards the garage. "It beder not be red! That's so cliché; I wann a orange car," he muttered with a mouthful of food. Anne watched from the kitchen window as Peter headed to the garage alone.

He trotted down the worn path. As he got closer to the garage, he noticed the side door was cracked opened. *Really? Did she tell me to go out here to just the door? She couldn't just shut the door herself?*

Reaching out to grab the door knob to pull it shut, he noticed movement and light inside. He stiffened, afraid of the shadows since childhood, then he hesitantly proceeded. "Hello," he called.

He pushed the door forward; something was stuck behind it. He leaned on the door to get it to open more, but it wouldn't go. He slipped in sideways, sucking in his already thin gut, he squeezed through the door and as his eyes adjusted to the light, he saw it . . .

Humungous, magnificent, and striking as always, he took in its' beauty. Peter had every curve memorized and every scratch etched forever into his brain. Exa's grand piano was standing before him. "I want to give it to you," Exa's voice came from a shadow in the corner. She stepped forward into the light with a frown on her face.

Peter fumbled still in awe as he swallowed the last of his sandwich. "No, I can't take your piano. It was a gift to you. It's worth more than some people's houses," He said as he licked off the last of the mayo that had stuck to his thumb.

"No, I never liked it. I saw it as more of a burden because it was always too bloody big to fit anywhere. But, you *adored* it from the first time you saw it; I adored watching you play it. My memory of this piano is watching you love it and watching you grow as you played it." Exa stepped closer to Peter. "I want you to have it."

"I don't know what to say."

"I'm proud of you, Pe ta. You're leaving on your first solo tour tomorrow. Look at all you have accomplished." Exa rested her hand on the piano. "This piano is you more than it is me."

Peter opened his mouth, and then closed it, then opened it again and said, "I guess . . ., thank you. You don't have to; you know you have given me enough. My whole career would never have happened without you."

"You're welcome, Pe ta. It's my pleasure. I wish that was the only thing I was here to tell you, but unfortunately, I also need to tell you goodbye. I'm moving." Her voice was flat as if she had rehearsed a speech.

Peter's attention shifted from the piano to Exa in alarm. "What? When?"

"Now. This piano was the last thing I needed to move out of my house. My landlord officially put my house on the market one hour ago. My movers left this morning with my belongings and I'll follow them right after I leave here." Exa swallowed hard.

"Where are you going?" Peter's eyebrows furrowed.

"I don't want say. I just need some privacy about that." Exa looked down.

"What do you mean you can't tell me?" Peter stepped forward to see Exa's face, but she turned her head.

"I'm at a point in my life where I need some space. I wish I could tell you, but I can't." Exa tried to say something else, but she couldn't get the words out. Taking a few more breaths, she started to speak again, "Pe ta, please don't end up like me. You need to live your life. You have an awesome talent and career, yes, but *don't* be like me."

"I don't understand," Peter said so softly that it was barely above a whisper.

"Don't just work. Don't forget to live . . . and to love," her voice cracked on the last word. "Pe ta, I adore you like a son, and please don't take this the wrong way, but we have spent so much time together over the years that I sometimes think you forgot to be a kid, have friends, and even date."

Peter shook his head and said, "I don't want those things. I like piano. I tried to have friends, but I wasn't a kid who liked to talk about Pokémon and XBOX. What other kid spends his weekends listening to Bach? And now, all the people my age just want to drink or talk about sports. I don't relate to anyone like I do you."

Exa's eyes met Peter's; she touched Peter's cheek. "I know sweetie. We're artists. The trouble is being an artist is like being in a one-sided love affair. You put all your energy into your art, but it can *never* love you back." Exa held Peter's gaze intensely for a moment, and then dropped it as she pivoted to face the piano with her back toward Peter. "Most artists end up being like me. *Please* Pe ta, don't let that happen to you."

"I don't get what you mean. What's wrong with being like you? People would die to have your career, your passion, your life. . ."

Exa turned to face Peter. "Look at me. I'm pushing forty, and I'm alone.

"You're married."

"Pe ta, when in the decade since we have known each other, have you seen me with my husband?" Exa's words were rambling and fast. "He's in Europe doing who bloody knows what, and the only reason we've not gotten a divorce is because it would be impossible to divide up all of our crap, not to mention the tabloid mess it would create. It's just easier to live separately and leave it as is," Exa's said as she was visibly upset.

"I'm sorry I brought it up. It's not my business," Peter cut her off, hoping to stop her from getting angrier. "I just don't understand why you can't tell me where you're going?" Peter touched her arm softly, "Please. . . Exa, you're my *person* – the only one that gets me."

"I did the public-life gig for 20 years; It broke me. I can't do it anymore. It's a prisoner's life. I just want to live in the shadows."

"Okay, I think I understand," Peter said as he knew to give up when Exa got upset. "But, thanks for everything, and just know that I'll really miss you. You know how to reach me if you want to."

Exa nodded, offered a hug, and walked out the door. Still confused, Peter watched as she walked away, feeling sad to lose his mentor and confidant of the past thirteen years. Turning back to the piano he loved, he pounded his fist hard on the keys. He sunk down onto the piano bench, hanging his head low, he breathed in the smell of the mahogany. It was a smell he knew, even with his eyes closed, and it brought a little serenity to him in that moment, but even that wasn't enough.

He wasn't sure how long he'd been sitting at the piano when he heard his mom's voice, "Honey, are you okay?" She was standing behind him.

"Yeah." He straightened up.

"Are you loving your piano? Exa asked me yesterday if she could sneak it over here, and I had the hardest time hiding it from you. You should have seen all those men struggling to get it back here. She had a whole crew . . ." Her voice trailed off as she saw Peter's face was flushed. "What's wrong? You don't like it?"

"It's not the piano. Exa's leaving, and she doesn't want me to know where she's going. She doesn't want me to hang out with her anymore. She thinks I need to get a life and some real friends," he said in a mocking tone.

Anne slid next to Peter on the bench and put her arm around him. "Well, we can't change her decision, but she may change it on her own later. I'm sorry she feels that way. I know it hurts you. Exa's important to our whole family." Anne meant what she said, too, as she really had come to love Exa like a family member. "Are you going to be able to play tonight?"

"I have to play. It's all I know." Peter half smiled at his mom.

"You know, there's a saying I love that goes like this, *'People come into your life for a reason, a season, or a lifetime'*. I think Exa was here for a reason; she led you to this amazing career. But tonight, you're starting a new journey by yourself. She knows you don't need her anymore."

"Maybe, it's still a shock though." Peter rubbed the whisker stubble on his chin. "I need to clear my head and get ready. Are you packed and ready for the tour?"

"I'm getting there."

"Yeah, me too. I need to get that done now so, I can think about something else. Will you come backstage before the show?"

"Yes, of course," Anne said.

* * *

In Peter's hospital room, Anne watched the clock on the wall. The minute hand made a faint ticking noise that everyone could hear because it was quiet. Anne sighed heavily, breaking the silence in Peter's hospital room, "Peter was upset about Exa. She moved, but she didn't want Peter to know where she was going because she said she needed some privacy.

Gwen nodded. "I can see how that would upset him."

"I think he tried to forget about it, but I know it will bother him. I think he'll always miss her," Anne said.

"That's too bad that she couldn't be a little more understanding of Peter's feelings, but I guess she has to live her life too."

"Yeah, and I told him she may change her mind," Anne added.

"Maybe. But, I know Peter's resting, and you must be exhausted too. I don't want to impose; I just wanted to stop for a second. Can you make sure he sees my flowers?" Gwen asked.

"Yeah, I will. It was so great to see you. I can text you when he wakes up," Anne said.

"I would like that." Gwen left the room as quietly as she had entered.

Peter heard their conversation. He wanted to tell Gwen not to leave and he was frustrated when he tried but couldn't speak. He was coming into a clearer state of consciousness, and he realized he had the ability to open his eyes. First he saw the ceiling, and then he looked to the left. He saw his mom and dad sitting next to him. He slid his hand over to the edge of the bed. "Tom, he's awake. Peter, can you hear me?" Anne shot to her feet with a smile so broad it almost didn't fit on her face.

Peter could hear them perfectly, but forming a word with his mouth was a different task. He felt like he had a bad case of cotton mouth it was so dry. Pressure behind his eyes created the most intense headache he had ever felt; it hurt to keep his eyes opened. He struggled, but everything seemed so bright. Anne noticed Peter trying to look around. "It's okay. Just rest," she said. The room seemed to get brighter, Peter closed his eyes. His head throbbed like daggers were being driven into it. He was unable to stand the pain, so he let his body drift back to sleep; he was just so tired.

Twenty-three

PETER

Later that night, Peter woke up with greater ability to focus, and he had questions. At first, Thomas and Anne tried to put off his questions, but as Peter became more alert, he was more insistent. Anne and Thomas felt like it was time to include him in on some of the details of his situation. It was a moment of crystal clarity for Peter; his focus was sharper than it had been in days, and he was ready to hear about his health.

"Just tell me what happened. It's my kidneys, right?" Peter asked. Anne's stomach felt like it jumped into her throat, and she couldn't speak. Peter turned toward his dad, but Thomas didn't say anything either.

Peter pressed, "Do I need a transplant? I do, don't I?" His eyes searched his parent's faces for any hint of confirmation.

Anne nodded and then looked to Thomas, waiting for him to explain.

"Yeah, you already know; it's time. Your kidneys can't do this anymore," Thomas said.

"Okay," Peter breathed. He had always known his kidneys were weak. He had heard about people having transplants before and knew it would be hard and painful, but worth it. He put on a brave face. "So . . . do I go on a list for a kidney, or how does that work?" He looked at his dad.

Thomas looked at Anne, and then shook his head as he turned back to Peter. "Son, you see, in some cases, that would be an option, but you need a match." He scratched his chin. "There's something called a PRA score; it ranges from zero to ninety-nine. A score of twenty-five would mean that twenty-five percent of the population will not be a match for you. The antibodies present in your blood would attack the kidney. Everyone has a different score, and it goes up if you have had trauma or surgeries in your life . . ."

Peter waited as his dad paused, then said, "I wish I had better news, but your score is over 98%." Thomas paused for a moment and then continued, "Your score means that out of a hundred people, less than two would be able to donate. There's also another risk that just because you find a match, it doesn't mean your body will take it, and it's a lot to put your body through if you don't have great odds." Thomas paused again, rubbing his chin again, and continued, "I don't think I've ever seen a score that high; it's because of all of your surgeries and your cerebral palsy. Your doctors think it's too risky to accept a kidney from anyone other than a direct family member, and possibly only a parent . . . preferably the mother," His voice trailed off as he waited for Peter to process the information.

"Well, that should be okay," Peter said hopefully as his gaze bounced from his dad to his mom.

"Peter, it's not that simple. If I could, I would give you my kidney in a heartbeat, but I can't," Thomas's voice cracked. Anne interrupted him, loudly sniffing back her own tears. She placed a hand on Thomas's leg, and quietly begged him, "Don't tell him. Please Tom, not like this."

"Tell me what?" Peter pressed.

"Please Tom, don't," she pleaded harder.

"Tell me what? Mom, you're scaring me."

"How can I not? We're at a dead end. Anne, he *needs* to know."

Thomas wiped his eye with the back of his hand. "What's your plan? I'm out of answers."

"Tell me what?" Peter begged again. Now he was scared because he'd never seen his dad cry before.

Anne reached out to touch Peter's face. She slid her hand down his cheek and rested her hand on his hand. Then she sat up straighter, took deep breaths, and stared directly into Peter's eyes. "I'll tell you. I'm your mother, and I'll tell you."

Thomas nodded. Anne's face was pale, but she continued, "Peter, I love you. *I love you* more than life itself. I've always done everything I could to protect you and be there for you, and I'll continue to do whatever's in my power. . . I have loved watching you grow. I have learned more from you than I could learn from any teacher. Please know that aside from anything I could ever tell you, you are so *loved*; you're such a gift."

"Mom, I know you love me; what do you have to tell me?" Peter's brain hurt from trying to solve this puzzle.

"This is an impossible conversation. Peter, we never wanted to have this secret from you. We just never knew when to tell you. You were too young, and then too sick. Then, you had all those issues not fitting in at school. We didn't want to make your home life more complicated. I wanted you to *truly* fit in somewhere. Your dad and I agreed to write a letter to give you on your eighteenth birthday, but you need to know a little sooner than what we had planned." Tears fell from Anne's eyes; her cheeks reddened as she wiped them with the back of her hand.

Peter waited. Anne grabbed both his hands, squeezing them hard. She said the words she never thought she could, "Peter, you're adopted."

At first, Peter didn't react. He kept looking to his mother to explain, but when he realized she didn't have any more words, he stuttered, "What?"

Both his parents nodded, and Peter fumbled for words. "So, like, how? What about Paul, and Tane, and Marie?"

"They're your siblings and always will be, as well as Shiloh, and the twins. But no, they're not adopted. You're the only child we adopted," Anne said.

"Now you tell me?" Peter whispered out of breath.

"Like I said, we were going to tell you in a few weeks when you turned eighteen. We just didn't want you to ever think you were less a part of our family. Peter, you mean the world to all of us." Anne dabbed the last of her tears away as she felt better now that she got the words out.

"Does everyone know?"

"No. All the kids, even your grandparents, everyone, they all think you were our birth child. I guess it's up to you if you want to tell them," Thomas said.

"Why all the secrecy?"

Thomas and Anne looked at each other, and Thomas shrugged his shoulders. "It's hard to understand, Peter. We did the best we could. We just didn't know what to do," Thomas said.

Peter, who was pale as his hospital sheets, drifted into deep thought exploring his childhood memories for clues, *I had no idea. I always felt loved, especially by my mother . . . I always felt like I was her favorite,* but then he stumbled on a memory that confused him. He turned to his mother, he said sheepishly, "I remember nursing."

Anne nodded her head, "Yep, I nursed you. I was able to get my milk back, and we nursed for a long time; I think you were almost two. It doesn't surprise me that you can remember it." She watched Peter's face and it seemed the special sparkle that he had in his eyes was being dimmed. "Peter, please don't over think this. We are your family – always have been and *always* will be. I'm sorry we didn't tell you sooner, but really, it's better this way."

"Do you know my birth parents?"

"Why?" Anne asked.

"Well, you just said if I don't get a kidney from my real parents, then I probably won't find one." Peter's bright blue eyes darkened even more as he was mentally connecting the dots. The shock of being adopted had delayed the connection about the kidney being unavailable, but now Peter saw his situation clearly.

Thomas spoke up, "Son, we sort of, um, went through the church for your adoption. Father Raymond helped us. But, uh, it was definitely a closed adoption."

"So, would he have a record? Would he be able to contact my birth parents just to see?" Peter leaned to look into his dad's eyes, but it was Anne who spoke.

"We can talk to him, and see what he says." She smiled, but it was obvious to Peter that it was a forced smile.

"Do you think I'm going to be okay?" His eyes darted between both of his parents.

Anne pulled Peter into an embrace. He could feel her body trembling. "Peter, we're gonna do our best. We haven't come this far to give up now," she said.

Twenty-four

After another week in the hospital, Peter was back resting at his parent's house under a strict dialysis schedule and light duty restriction. On that first morning home, Peter paced across his room constantly, checking his cell phone for a message from his dad who was supposed to be talking to Father Raymond about his adoption. *I just can't wait any longer or I'll lose my mind.* He tossed his phone onto his bed and flopped down next to it, stretching out on his back, folding his arms behind his head.

The crack near the ceiling caught his attention. He followed it as it drew a boundary in the light-blue paint between the window and closet, stopping at a photograph on the wall. It was a picture of Exa and him at Radio City Music Hall in New York City. It was right after they had finished playing an encore that night. *I think I was maybe fourteen in that picture. I was pretty short standing next to Exa. I'm taller than she is now. It really wasn't that long ago. My future was so promising back then. Now it's all joke.* He rolled onto his side so he didn't have to look at the picture of him smiling. *That kid was a fool.* He yawned. *Maybe it's my meds, but I'm exhausted.* Peter closed his eyes and felt the muscles in his face relax. His breathing steadied as he fell asleep into a dream.

It started with a bird's-eye view of a dark hollow room with bare walls and wooden floors that sat empty except for a small, white rocking-baby cradle in the middle of the room. His view zoomed in, and he saw a window open; the linen curtain danced in the breeze. The smell of fresh-cut grass wafted in through the window.

Peter heard a baby cry. He looked around the room. He was now walking in the room with bare feet on the wood floor. The cries got louder and more intense, sparking a feeling of panic in Peter's chest as he searched for the noise. It was coming from the cradle, which now rocked, back and forth on its own. Peter leaned over the cradle to pick up the baby to console it, but the cradle was empty. The cries got louder and more intense. The cradle rocked faster, but there was still no baby.

Peter touched the cradle to try to stop it. *Ouch!* It burned Peter's hand; he jumped back, and he heard laughing. The wind gusted in from the window. The room started spinning as he backed away from the cradle towards the door. The wind blew harder, and it held Peter back. The room spun faster, and the door moved away from Peter. Peter pivoted to chase after the door, but the room spun even faster, and the door moved faster while the wind blew at him. Peter ran after the door, but he couldn't keep up. The laughing got louder, ringing of insanity. "I want out of here!" he cried out. A thundering sound shook the house, and everything stopped; it was silent.

The dream continued with a bright light shining through the window. The door blew open, and the Goat Woman emerged in the doorway! She was holding something – a baby.

His mind slammed back into focus as he awoke. His stomach heaved in disgust as he focused on his breath. *It was just a dream,* he told himself as he sat straight up in bed. *But it's not just a dream, there's something more. . . I just can't see it.* He rubbed his head, but nothing came to him; it was blocked. He climbed out of bed and removed his sweat-soaked t-shirt. He replaced it with another identical grey t-shirt. *I need answers now;* he went to find his mom.

Peter found Anne making coffee in the kitchen while the twins sat at the table eating pancakes with strawberry topping. "Mom, we need to talk. I need to know. I can't live like this anymore. I keep having nightmares." Peter's eyes pleaded with his mother. Anne looked down at her coffee cup in her hand, and then looked back up at him.

"Call your dad," she said.

An hour later, Thomas picked them up in Anne's van. Shiloh had agreed to watch the twins, so Anne could go along, too. The three of them headed to the church to meet with Father Raymond.

I have to know who my birth parents are. I need their help. I would think if they knew I was desperate for a kidney, they would have to help me. I just need a name – anything. I would even pay them. I have money, lots of it. Peter's mind raced as they drove. Thomas parked the van and Peter bolted out towards the rectory; his parents jogged to keep up. "Peter, take it easy, please," Anne said as she followed behind him with his cane. Peter ignored her and was already walking through the door.

Jeannie, the church secretary, was in her office and greeted them, "Hi, Father's in the meeting room over there. He's expecting you." Peter busted through the door, and then stopped dead in his tracks. His face fell and tighten. In the board room sat Father Raymond, as expected, but next to him was the face of someone who tormented him his whole life – the Goat Woman. Older now, and practically hunched over, her green eyes confirmed it was definitely her.

In a trance, Peter shook his head back and forth as he inched back towards the door, not letting his eyes off her. Something magnetic in her pulled him toward her. "No, no, no," Peter repeated over as he continued to ease back towards the exit door.

"Peter, calm down. Do you need to sit? Tom, get him a chair," Anne said.

"I'm not sitting!" Peter snapped.

"You're not well son; sit for a minute," Thomas said.

"Why is she here?" Peter pointed, his eyes locked on her.

Father Raymond spoke up, "I asked her to come here to help explain your adoption."

"No, no," Peter insisted. "You're not going to tell me she's my birth mom! All my life you have haunted me! What did I ever do to you?" He pivoted, looking back at his parents, he continued, "Are you people really going to bring me in here to tell me she's my mother?"

Anger surged in his veins; he wanted answers, but nobody dared speak until, finally, a voice he had heard only in dreams meekly said, "Peter, I know you're scared of me. Please stay, and let me explain." The Goat Woman pleaded, her voice so innocent and feminine sounding it seemed fake. Peter's curiosity coerced him to stay.

"You have one minute." Peter glared back at her, but his eyes periodically darted toward the exit.

The Goat Woman looked to Father, and then to Anne before speaking, "My name's Sarah. I live in . . ."

"You *know* I know where you live," Peter interrupted.

She looked down at her hands folded in front of her on the table and continued, "I know you saw me through the window that night. I don't know *exactly* what you saw, but I know you saw me and it scared you." She looked up again.

"What I saw? I saw you washing blood off your hands and trying to dispose of bloody sheets," Peter blurted out as he shook from the memory.

"What?" Anne asked looking to Thomas, and then back to Peter. "What are you talking about Peter?"

Ignoring his mom, Peter nodded to Sarah, "Go on. You have 30 seconds left."

"Okay, so . . . I work with the church. I'm a nun."

Peter snorted, "A nun? You don't look like a nun."

"I don't wear my habit because I have a different mission here, and I don't want to draw attention to it. I came here a little over twenty-years ago to help do outreach work for pregnancy- crisis situations." She paused, looked to Anne, and asked, "How much do you want me to say?"

Thomas took the cue and slowly started to speak, "Peter, what you are about to hear is really grueling. We never meant to lie to you, but only to protect you. I can't explain what happened back then. I have wrestled with the "what-if's" your whole life. The only thing I have come to know is, sometimes, events line up perfectly like the stars in a constellation for a reason, and it is done by God's design. There were no accidents that day."

"You're not making any sense, dad. Don't speak so vaguely. Just tell me the truth," Peter interrupted.

"I will. Let me start at the beginning, but sit down first." Peter reluctantly sat and Thomas took a seat across from Peter and Anne sat next to him. Thomas went on, "The day you were born, I was working overnight at the hospital. The church just started their medical outreach program to the Indian reservations. They had this older ambulance donated to them and we stocked it with medical supplies. Two times a month, we drove it to the reservation to perform free medical services.

Sometimes, we had a dentist with us or some nurses. The details of how we ran the program back then were very rough and all volunteer. I was the only doctor who took the time to go, so it was busy for me. I never had the option of skipping a visit because without a doctor on the truck, we couldn't officially call it a medical mission. Usually, Father would try to come to help with spiritual counseling. We took all the help we could get," Thomas paused.

Anne spoke next, "Your father usually had a nurse help him, but that day there wasn't anyone available. He was exhausted from working all night and in no position to drive, but he couldn't call in sick. I volunteered to go with him to drive, so he could nap on the way down. I know how to take someone's blood pressure and help with forms. Your father told me I should meet everyone across the street at the clinic where Sarah had the mission truck waiting for us." Anne looked at Father, who began his recollection.

"The plan had been for me to pick everyone up, but I got called to do some other crisis counseling. I knew Sarah was on her way over to the clinic, so I asked her to take the truck and if she could go in my place to help with counseling. I was still going to try to make it, but I didn't want to hold up the show . . . Father looked to Sarah, who continued.

"Every Friday, I went to the clinic to pray. It used to be an abortion clinic, but there was never a local abortionist. They had one fly in every Friday from down south. They couldn't perform the abortions in the hospital because it was a Christian hospital, so the clinic was located right next to the hospital – in case emergency care was ever needed after a procedure.

It was a hot day and sort of slow. The regular nurse didn't show up, so they had a new travel nurse who I didn't know." She paused, looked to Anne who looked at Peter.

Peter was silent, waiting for the point of this long drawn out story as Anne continued, "I arrived and saw Sarah praying. She said a woman had gone in for an operation. It made me sad, so I started to pray, too. Your father showed up at the same time as Father Raymond."

Thomas interjected, "I knew, since they were both praying that someone was inside, and I knew your mother or Sarah wouldn't want to leave yet. A couple of minutes passed. The back door opened, and the nurse came out. She was. . ." Thomas stopped. "It was . . ." He shook his head.

Father spoke and summarized the next events as best he could, "Peter, she had a garbage bag. She looked at us and said, 'If you believe in God, ask him what he wants you to do about this one – he's alive'. She set the bag on the trashcan and went inside."

Everyone watched Peter. No one wanted to go into further details. Peter shook his head, he had to hear the words to believe it, "Then, what happened?"

Thomas spoke, "Inside the garbage bag was a baby – a fully-developed one, struggling to get air; it was you." Thomas looked at Peter, who had a deer-in-the-headlights expression on his face. "Your mother tried to abort you by a saline abortion, but you obviously came out alive, severely burned, but alive. You couldn't breathe on your own, so I cleaned out your airway and grabbed a ventilator out of the truck." Thomas rubbed the back of his neck.

"I don't know what you are saying," Peter said. His breathing was heavy, and he was dizzy. *This is so messed up.*

"I wanted to run into the hospital and grab a whole team of doctors to help save you, but I knew it would backfire because you were supposed to be . . . dead. Normally, when an abortion fails, the abortionist will finish the job. Occasionally a baby survives an abortion, and the doctor must sign the birth certificate. I knew, since your mother's doctor made the nurse take you away, that he was not a doctor who was going to sign your birth certificate or be glad we tried to redeem you." Thomas grimaced and continued, "You can stop me anytime. You don't need to hear all this."

Peter felt hollow now. He was past the point of shock; he was numb. He needed to know. "Go on," he insisted.

"We didn't want anyone to see you, so we piled into the mission truck. I examined you, and you were perfect – beautiful. You were fighting to live. I learned in medical school that the best incubator is a mother's chest. Her chest will raise its' temperature to heat her baby, so to help warm you, Anne held you. I could see by the look on her face that she bonded with you instantly."

Anne spoke again, "I held you and it seemed like you were getting stronger. We had to make a decision." Anne tried to grab Peter's hand, but he jerked it away. "Peter, do you understand, now?"

Peter was stunned. All his childhood truths as he had known them were gone. *I'm living a life full of lies.* "No, I don't. Then, what happened," he asked.

Thomas continued, "We had minimal supplies on the truck to clean you up and clot your burns. We all pledged to do what we could to save you and that meant keeping a secret and even fabricating some lies. We had one major problem though."

"What?" Peter asked.

"We couldn't let anyone know where you came from because we could go to jail for kidnapping. We had to find a place to keep you safe and come up with a believable back story. We couldn't take you to our house because we had nosey kids. Father couldn't care for you in the church either, so Sarah volunteered her little cabin."

"I took you home with me," Sarah confirmed.

Peter rubbed his forehead hoping it would help him to hear her words differently. He glared at his mom, "How could you keep this from me? You knew I was terrified of her."

Anne looked to the floor. "Peter, what choice did I have? It wouldn't have made sense to tell you one part without telling you everything. I was always going to tell you, but when the timing was better." Anne's voice squeaked.

Sarah cleared her throat to speak again, "I took you home with me to live in my cabin. You needed to be fed, and formula wasn't going to work for your premature digestive system. Your mom was pumping breast milk and would even come to nurse you, but I needed something to supplement it. Goat's milk has long been known to have the closest properties to human milk and with a little, extra, vitamin supplementation, it works well once you dilute it. I got a couple of milking goats, so I had fresh milk for you.

"You gave me goat's milk?" Peter interrupted.

Nodding her head, Sarah continued. "So, people started calling me The Goat Woman because I had goats at my house. The goats I had were all because of you. I told people I was using the milk to make and sell soap to support my mission."

Peter looked up to the ceiling in disbelief, but Sarah continued. "So, before this all happened, children would always play around my cabin. They loved rolling on the hill on sunny days, and I always spoiled them with treats. It got worse when I got the goats; whole families would congregate on my hill after church to pet and feed the goats. I had to do something to make sure the kids didn't see anything or hear your cries. We couldn't let anyone have even a tiny clue about what was going on. So, I made up scary stories to tell the kids in the area, so they would stay away from my house. I made sure every kid knew the stories, and it worked. So, all the stories you probably have heard about the Goat Woman, I made them up – to protect you."

"Stop," Peter held up his hand. "I need to think. You're telling me I wasn't even adopted, but you stole me from the trash," he winced as he spoke.

"You're a survivor, Peter. I know it sounds hard to believe. Why do you think we couldn't tell you when you were little?" Anne pleaded as she tried to grab Peter's hand again, but he shook her off. "It's the truth, I swear. It kills me to have to tell you this."

"So, then what? Did you just bring me home one day?"

Anne spoke, "Sort of. We knew you were premature, so your dad and I agreed I would wear a pregnancy pillow for a while to show I was carrying a baby. We waited for you to get stronger. We had no idea if you were going to make it. We just took everything one day at a time."

Thomas spoke again, "When I determined you were strong enough to come home, we told people your mom went into labor, and it went so fast that she delivered right at home. It was pretty simple. I filled out the paper work for a birth certificate, just like I would if she had delivered in the hospital. If it had been anyone else, they would have required us to show a placenta from a home birth. Everyone trusted us because they *saw* she had been pregnant. Then we took you home."

Anne reached for Peter's hand again, and this time he let her take it. "Please forgive us. We didn't know what to do. We just wanted to love you as long as you were here, so you would not be afraid. We received the biggest blessing of all . . . you."

Peter's brain was throbbing. *This pull I have to the Goat Woman was because I really did have a connection to her — she raised me when I was a baby.* "Why couldn't you just go back and tell the doctors I was alive?" Peter asked. "Don't you take an oath as a doctor to protect life?"

"There are no protection laws for something like this. Your birth mother signed the papers to abort you so that is what the doctor was required to do. For us to keep you alive was a crime. Really, the travel nurse saved your life because she didn't do her job to correct the error," Thomas explained.

Sarah spoke, "I always felt protective of you. I've watched over you. I know you saw me watching you a few times, and it scared you. I never meant to scare you. I just have always loved you from a distance."

Peter placed his hands on the sides of his head and pushed on his temples to stop a stress headache from coming on. *This is all beyond messed up. I can't even believe it.*

Thomas spoke again, "Peter, as you started to grow, we saw some issues. We took you to specialists when you were around the age of one. He diagnosed you with cerebral palsy. You know about your disability, but what you don't know is that doctors determined it was caused by the lack of oxygen to your brain at birth. Your disability is because of the procedure."

"I always wondered why I had to be different. I swore it was God's punishment for something I did," Peter said and he started to cry. Time passed, and he cried harder. Pulling himself together, he faced his parents to ask the one question, no one wanted to answer, "So, you're telling me that you don't know who my birth mother is. She doesn't even know I'm alive. She thinks she already killed me, and there's no kidney for me?" Matching eyes with his dad, Thomas couldn't answer. Thomas stood up and grabbed his son in an embrace, and Anne met them both as they cried together.

Twenty-five

Peter emotionally detached that night. *I cannot care anymore. This life has been lived.* He sat at his newly gifted piano in his dark garage, with only a few candles glowing on top so, he could see the keys. Peter played "The Goat Woman" song he knew from memory over and over. Hours passed, and Peter played. Anne walked in with a sandwich and cold lemonade, his favorite drink, but he never looked up. To Anne, it appeared Peter made every effort to specifically ignore her. She laid the sandwich on the piano, squeezed his shoulder, and left him alone, but it killed her to be disconnected from him.

An alarmed beeped on Peter's phone. He silenced the ringer. *Dialysis Appointment. No point in doing that anymore. I'm never getting a kidney. I'm not dragging out this misery.*

The door creaked as it opened. It was dark outside; no light crept in through the door to help Peter steal a glimpse of who was coming into his garage, but he really didn't care. *There's zero point in caring about anything when it's all going to be over soon.* Footsteps stopped behind him. *I don't know what that smell is. It's sweet like fresh rain.* He looked up, and jumped to his feet when he saw it was the Goat Woman. Sarah, as he now knew her, was standing behind him.

"Sarah! You scared me to death. You know I'm not used to thinking of you as a normal person." Peter held his chest.

"Sorry, your mom said you were back here, but I already knew. I've watched you play down here a lot of nights," Sarah admitted.

"Now you openly admitting to stalking me. That's creepy." Peter stepped back.

"I've watched you only in a way a mother watches her child, but I never wanted to get caught," she smiled.

"So, now you are just going to come right in to hang out?"

"No, I'm here because I have something for you. I mean, I don't have it here right now, but we can go get it. It should help you."

"Go, get what now?"

"It's sort of a secret, and your parents don't even know about it. I was hoping we could sneak out and be back in an hour or so. I have my car out front. Come ride with me?"

"You do know up until a few hours ago, I was terrified of you. Now, I'm supposed to get in a car with you without even telling my parents."

"Well, do you think they would let you go in your condition?"

"Good point. Where are we going?" Peter grabbed his sweatshirt that he had draped over the piano bench.

"We're going to go to my cabin, but then take a walk to find something. You can say 'No', but I think you'll want to see it."

Peter thought for a second, *I don't really have anything to lose.* "Okay, why not?" He slipped his sweatshirt over his head and blew out the candles on the piano. Smoke lingered in a stream that captured both of their attentions. After a few moments of watching the smoke dissipate, they left in silence.

Sarah drove to her house. "I didn't forget about this, but I just needed you to have some time to process what you were hearing this morning. It was a lot to hear, wasn't it?"

"Um, yeah it was a little much," Peter couldn't mask the pain in his voice.

Sarah thumped her fingers on the steering wheel, "Your parents love you so much. I think they just did the best they could with what they had." She turned the car into the parking area in front of her cabin, shut it off, and opened her door. She motioned for Peter to get out.

Sliding his foot out the door, Peter kicked something on the floorboard, and it fell out onto the ground. He leaned over to retrieve it, and he recognized it immediately. It was a copy of his *Goat Woman* CD, his first single, released almost eight years ago when he was only ten-years-old. Blushing, Sarah grabbed it back, "Sorry, I'm not the neatest person – especially in my car. I could never resist a Goat Woman CD." A sly smile crept on her face as she chucked the CD case back into the car and shut the door.

Peter looked at Sarah as if seeing her for the first time; she looked embarrassed. "Are you strong enough to follow me on foot, or should we go grab Father's four wheeler?" she asked, wanting to change the subject.

"Yeah, I can walk."

"Don't you need your cane?"

Peter glanced sideways at Sarah, "You would know I use a cane," he kicked the dirt beneath his feet. *I know this walking path. It's steep but I really don't care about my health, not anymore.* "I don't need it," Peter said and then took off ahead of her up the hill. They hiked slowly to allow Peter to pace himself.

"Can I ask you something?" Sarah asked.

"Sure."

"I know that when you were little, you believed all the "Legends-of-the-Goat-Woman" stuff the other kids told you, but . . . you had to stop believing it as some point, I mean it was like Santa Claus. How come you were still afraid of me?"

Peter chewed his bottom lip as he thought about her question. "I guess it probably has to do with the whole bloody-sheets episode I saw at your cabin. What were you doing?" Peter looked sideways at her.

"Perfect timing for your question as I'm about to show you."

They reached the peak of the hill and started to go into the wooded area. Near an opening into a path was a huge tree trunk with a shovel leaning against it. Peter reached the stump first and leaned on it to rest. *I really overestimated my strength.*

Sarah reached the stump, grabbed the shovel, and kept walking; Peter traipsed behind her. Sarah carried a little flashlight she had grabbed out of her car, and it was just enough to light their path. They reached the end of the trail, and there was a large brown rock. Sarah threw the shovel down, propped her hands on the rock, and leaned her whole body into it. "Are you trying to move that?" Peter asked. "It's half your size."

"Yeah, can you help me?" Dead serious and fixed on the task at hand, she didn't look up. Peter leaned over onto the rock, and they pushed together.

"Maybe we can roll it?" Peter questioned. "I can put the shovel underneath it, and try to lift it a little?"

"Okay, here, let me do that," Sarah said as she grabbed the shovel, and the two of them rolled the rock the tiniest inkling over, so that the ground it had been resting on was now exposed.

Sara stood up straight to catch her breath. She regained her composure and began to dig into the ground. "Are we looking for buried treasure?" Peter raised an eyebrow.

"To you, this will be better than gold," She said as she dug a rather large hole into the ground. Her shovel hit something. She bent over, brushed the dirt off with her hands, and wiggled it out of the dirt as Peter shown the flashlight on it.

"It's a wooden box," Peter said. *I've seen that box before.* It was identical to the one Sarah had on her counter the night he looked in her window.

Sarah brushed off the last of the dirt, and pushed the box towards Peter. "Open it."

"Are you nuts?" *Should I even get my finger prints on it? I'm not getting sucked into your crime scene.*" Peter's eyes squinted with suspicion.

"Open it. Here give me the flashlight, and I'll help you see what's in here." Sarah said as they traded possessions.

"What is it?" Peter was hesitant to open it. He played with the edge of the lid, afraid to open it.

"It's your future," Sarah held his gaze.

"My future of being buried in a wooden box? Thanks for the encouragement."

"Open it," Sarah repeated as she shined the light on the box lid.

Peter glided the lid off and peered inside. Rolling around in the bottom of the box were two orange bottles with white lids, like prescriptions bottles. Peter picked one up; the label was faded and hard to read. However, he could make it out, "Zoloft." He arched his eyebrow. "You think I'm depressed?"

Sarah covered Peter's hand as he held the bottle. She clasped the bottle between her thumb and her index finger and rotated the bottle just slightly. "Now read it," she urged.

"Take one pill every twenty-four hours, I can't see the rest of it, and over here it says, Elizabeth Jurgens," Peter shrugged his shoulders. "What's the point of this?"

Sarah placed her finger so it held onto the word "Elizabeth". "That's her."

"Who?"

"Your mother."

All Peter heard was white noise. "What?"

"That's your mother's name."

"My mother's Elizabeth Jurgens. How do you know?" His chest tightened as he spoke.

"Yeah, it's crazy; I know. Here, first sit down. This will take a while." Sarah leaned against the rock and motioned for Peter to rest next to her. Peter timidly leaned onto the rock. *It does feel good to sit.*

Sarah looked up. The night sky was black and clear with stars hovering over them. Peter followed her gaze and focused on the stars. *Their stillness is overwhelming. In a world that never slows, everything is frozen up there. I bet if they looked down at us, they would get dizzy from our tempo.*

"So, Peter, do you remember when your dad said the nurse came out with the garbage bag?" Peter nodded. "It was a garbage bag; there was garbage in the bag, too. Your father handed it to me and told me to get rid of it. Something told me to look inside first. There wasn't much there, but somehow, in the bottom, I found these bottles."

"So. . . you found trash. How'd you know it belonged to my mother?"

"I didn't at first, but I just had this gut feeling. I mean, I knew it came from her room. I'm not going to say anymore because this is your journey, but Peter, I've been watching over you throughout your whole life. I've seen this play out. God has really been working in your life. It's her. I know it is."

Peter was no longer able to read her name because tears blurred it, but he didn't need to read it. He had his mother's name burned into his memory forever. "So, you buried it out here under a rock?"

"That's another long story. I didn't know what to do with it. I kept it in a shoebox in my house for a long time but it sort of crept me out. But, then something happened. Father became obsessed with checking the garbage bags from the clinic. Every time they did an abortion, the trash would come out of the room. He had to know what happened to the baby. He just couldn't forget about it. I think once you find one alive, you can't dismiss it.

"We never found another baby, of course, but we always found something pointing to one; whether it was a mother's ID bracelet or medical instructions, etc. We just didn't know what to do with the clues, and it seems so callous just to throw the stuff away. It was usually all that was left to represent an entire life. Over time, as Father was dumpster diving, he made friends with the nursing director. He found out they usually sent the babies to be harvested for body parts, which was illegal."

"What?" Peter interrupted. "That's disgusting."

Sarah continued, "It's sad. That's what it really is. Upon doing more research, we found there was a whole ring of doctors that did this sort of thing, and everyone on the inside was told to lie about it. Father tried to report the doctor but no one took him serious. Eventually, the abortionist made some sort of a deal that even I don't know the details of, but I know, in the end, they said Father could have the babies. He couldn't stand thinking that the babies never had proper burials. It really became his mission in life to make sure they were laid to rest." Sarah stood up, walked closer to the edge of the hill, still looking over the trees. She motioned for Peter to join her. Peter wobbled over to the ledge and looked out, too, not sure of what he was looking for.

"He brings the babies up here and together we bury them. We knew we couldn't go around digging holes in the ground all the time without people getting suspicious. To conceal the grave sites, we plant trees over them. . ." Her voice trailed off, she paused for a moment and then she continued, "Here they are. We call it our 'Cherub Garden'."

Peter looked out into the sea of evergreens; it went out past the skyline and appeared to be never-ending. "There have to be hundreds, if not thousands — it's a whole forest," Peter said.

"2,027. We've been working this mission for almost eighteen years. It adds up, you know. To me, the trees are a visual reminder of what we have lost."

"There were 2,027 abortions here in the last eighteen years?" Peter asked in disbelief.

"2,028. One got away." Sara winked at Peter. "So, after we started this memorial project, I still had your box of stuff. I couldn't throw it away because I just had this gut feeling. Something told me you might need it someday. You were special though. We didn't give you a tree because you got to live, so you got this rock."

"This makes me sick." Peter covered his mouth as his chin quivered. "Why would you guys do all this and have all these secrets?"

"How could we not do it? This has been my mission so long I don't even know what other people do. Father Raymond and I will probably be doing this until we die. We just can't stop checking the garbage."

"I was always told these trees were planted for the Christmas-wreath project. You're telling me these trees are holes you made because they're gravesites?"

"Yeah. The Christmas-wreath project is just a secondary use of the trees – sort of a cover up. We have to buy the trees. The budget committee was starting to get suspicious why we needed so many, so we came up with the fundraiser idea. Now, it more than pays for itself and further funds my mission here."

Peter watched the wind dance in the trees, inhaling the cool summer breeze; pine scent filled his lungs. *How could something so beautiful and strong like a tree be symbolic of something so, so . . . not.* "Do you think if people could see it, it would be different?"

Sarah shook her head and folded her lips in tight. "Over 58,000,000 babies just in our country. I don't think we could make a forest that big. It does seem like it's one of those things that people accept because they have been taught to accept it without actually *looking* at it," Sarah bit her lip. "So, Elizabeth Jurgens. You need to google her. Let's get out of here, so we can get some cell-phone service."

Peter was shocked by how hast he forgot he had astounding news and work to do. He hustled back to the car and started searching for Elizabeth Jurgens on his phone. "There are at least a hundred Elizabeth Jurgens's, but none in this area –except for a few old addresses from twenty-years ago. She must've moved out of area. What if she got married and changed her name? There has to be a way to narrow it down?" Peter said.

"We need to find a middle initial. Tomorrow, we should go request birth records for any in this area to see what her middle initial is to narrow it down. I can help you," Sarah said.

"Thank you," Peter looked at Sarah and for the first time he felt no fear. He felt the mother's love she had always had for him.

Sarah felt the connection too; it was a connection she had longed for, for many years. "You're welcome."

Twenty-Six

The next morning Peter decided to make up his missed dialysis appointment. He watched his blood filter out of his arm through a tube. *This really puts the frailty of life on display.* A text message beeped on his phone.

"*Are you up?*" It was Sarah.

"*Ya, I had to get my blood sucked out this morning☺*"

"*How long does that take?*"

"*IDK, hey, how did you get this number?*"

"*LOL I have my ways.*"

Peter scratched his head wondering about Sarah's resourcefulness.

"*So, what are you up to?*" Peter texted.

"*I found her.*"

Peter called her. His chest pounded. "Hey, you found Elizabeth. How?"

"I'm a nun. I have some advantages. I looked in the church archives for a baptism record. I thought, this is such a small community, and maybe she belonged to our church at some time, and bingo. I found someone who would be about that age and her middle name was Catherine. I didn't see any marriage records though. So, I did some more digging. I called the post office. Apparently, there's an Elizabeth C. Jurgens, who just registered with the post office. She must have moved recently. I have an address."

"No kidding! You have an address." Peter stretched his neck out to look for a nurse to come pull his dialysis cord out of him. *I sort of have a better place to be, lady.* He waved a nurse down in the hall. She smiled, and then continued to type on her computer. Peter winced with impatience.

"Yeah, and I would think it's current. Do you want me to pick you up, or should I give you the address?"

"Just give me the address."

"892 Swan Lane."

Peter knew that area of town as it was 'the' most affluent neighborhood, which made his heart sink a little. *She's probably a rich snob.*

"Thanks. I'll let you know how it goes."

"Good luck," Sarah said, "Bye."

Another thirty minutes passed before the nurse had Peter ready to leave. Not knowing if it was hospital policy, or just his parent's policy, he was told not to drive after dialysis, so he had to wait for a ride. Anne was parked in the handicapped spot right out front. Peter had a somber expression on his face when he climbed into the van; Anne picked it up right away. "What happened? Are you dizzy? Put your head down a bit."

"No mom, I'm not dizzy. I have something to tell you. I wanted to tell you this morning, but everyone else was there. Last night, Sarah came to visit me."

"I knew that."

"She told me she had something for me, and we went to her cabin."

"You left?"

"I did. She gave me this box, and in it were some pills with a name on it. She apparently took it out of the trash bag where you found me and she thinks the pills were my birth mom's. There's a name on the bottle. Sarah did some research and she texted me with an address, and so we found her, mom; we found my birth mom," Peter blurted it out, not believing it himself!

"How? I mean, you just told me how, but she had these pills this whole time?"

Peter pulled the bottle out of his pocket and gave it to his mom. She rolled it over slowly, reading it. She covered her mouth with one hand. "Oh, wow, Peter. What if this is her? It's a miracle."

"Don't get your hopes up. I still don't know what I will say to her. What if she denies she had an abortion? How do I even bring it up?"

"I don't know what to say," Anne admitted. "If it were me, I would be excited to see you. Maybe you shouldn't mention the kidney right away. Maybe just tell her who you are and see how that goes."

"No, duh, mom, I'm not going to ask her for a kidney. I know what NOT to say, but really, what *do* I say? I can't just say, I know you had an abortion, and it's me and I'm alive –

surprise."

"Okay, let's stop being sarcastic here. Let's practice. I'll be her and you be you, and be real," Anne said.

"No, I'm not doing that. It's dumb, mom. This is serious. There's no way anyone could walk up to someone and start talking about this stuff."

"What if you went there to introduce yourself, so you can see who she is . . . If she's nice and if it feels right, you could hand her a letter explaining everything," Anne offered.

"A letter," Peter thought. "Yeah, that's perfect. Do you want to help me write it?"

"Yeah, I can. When do you want to work on it?"

"Now, mom. I don't have time. I need to do all this yesterday."

"Okay, um here, look in the backseat, I have some notebooks back there from the twins. I'll rip out those first color pages. Here's a good page," Anne narrated as she handed Peter the notebook. "I have a pen in my purse too." Anne dug into her purse, pulled out a fountain pen, and handed it to Peter.

"What should I write, mom?" Peter starred at the blank page.

"How about, 'Dear Elizabeth Jurgens'."

Peter glared at his mom, "Wow, that's original. Okay. I have it from here."

Dear Elizabeth:

My name is Peter Arnold. I grew up here in Mara Gap and had the best family. I recently found out that I had been adopted and there were complications to my adoption; it was not a legal adoption. My parents found me in the trash can at Cedar Clinic on July 3rd, seventeen years ago – the result of an unsuccessful abortion. I have been in touch with one of the witnesses that was there, and she has reason to believe you are the woman who had the procedure.

I'm reaching out to you today only because I want to know you. I'm not angry. I have had the best life and best family. I understand this is shocking, so please take some time to think about it and call me at the number on the bottom if you care to talk further.

Thanks kindly,

Peter Arnold.

"How does that sound?" Peter asked. "Corny?"

"I think no matter what you write it's going to sound weird because the situation's weird." They nodded in agreement to each other. "Now what?" Anne asked. "Do you want to mail it?"

"No mom. I want to take it there now. I can't risk mailing it, and her not getting it, and then I'll never know."

"Okay, we can go there now. I just want to make sure that you're ready. This happened fast." Anne grabbed Peter's hand . . . "I mean it. Are you ready for this? It could turn out badly. You're going to bombard her with this. Be prepared."

"I know what you're saying, mom. I get it." Peter looked out his window. "But, I have to try." Anne cranked the key to start the van, reversed it, and drove across town. Peter watched the houses pass outside his window; the closer they got the bigger the houses became.

Anne pulled up to the curb and stopped in front of a stucco-French-country-style house with the matching address. She turned to Peter, she said, "This is your moment. You make sure you're ready; we can sit here as long as you need."

"I can't wait any longer," Peter said as he pulled the handle back on the door to open it.

"I'll be right here waiting for you," Anne reached over to hug her son. "I love you Peter and know however this goes, you are loved by me," Anne said with a reassuring smile. But, her insides were twisting, begging Elizabeth not to break her son's heart.

Peter slid out of the van and walked up the sidewalk. A beautiful weeping willow shaded the driveway on one side, creating a shadow on the house. His heart pounded. He was excited and scared, but nervous and hopeful; he reached the steps. He knocked on the door.

He heard footsteps. *Breathe. Don't forget to talk when you see her.* Licking his lips to keep his mouth from sticking shut, he shifted back on his feet. He reached out and placed a hand on the wall to brace himself. With his other hand, he touched his pocket for the letter; it was there. *I can do this.*

The door swung open wide, and he could see inside. A face moved closer to the screen door and as it moved, Peter captured it like a picture he had seen a million times. He knew every line of her smile, every twinkle of her brilliant, blue eyes, for he had seen them a thousand times. All the fear he had before knocking was gone the moment he laid eyes on her.

Out of the now-open door, she spoke in the beautiful voice Peter loved, "Pe ta, how did you find me?" For the voice belong to none other than Peter's beloved Exa Scarletta.

The End

Special
Bonus Offer

Thank you for reading Ruby in the Water. Would you like to read what happens next?

Download a FREE chapter to "Lily in the Stone", the sequel book to "Ruby in the Water" at http://www.jpsterlingauthor.com/free/

Ruby in the Water Book Club Questions

Were you immediately drawn into the story—or did it take a while? Did the book intrigue, amuse, disturb, alienate, irritate, or entertain you?

Consider Anne: What motivates her? Is there anything you find confusing about her? How does she grow during the story?

If you had to pick one scene with Anne that would encapsulate her character, which one would you pick and why?

Do you support Anne's and Thomas's decision to homeschool Peter? Why or why not?

What kind of husband would you describe Thomas to be? Did you find him likable?

What are Peter's primary characteristics? Which characteristics about Peter do you like or dislike?

Thomas described Peter to have the characteristics of "high sensitively", but through-out the book he proves to have more connection to his subconscious memories. Have you ever had an experience where you've felt something deeper? Perhaps a dream, or conversation or song?

Mrs. Polly described Peter's love of music as his "life boat" for all rest of the yucky stuff in life. What is your "life boat" in life that helps you get through the hard stuff?

Describe one passage or scene that lingers with you. Does it strike you as insightful, funny, odd, or profound? Perhaps a bit of dialog that's funny or poignant or that encapsulates a character? Maybe there's a particular comment that states the book's thematic concerns?

What motivates Exa? Do find her actions to be justified or ethical? Do you like or dislike her?

Do you see Exa change as the book goes on? If so how?

Consider Peter's second dream about the Goat Woman where he is in the house with the empty cradle. Describe some of the symbolism you see that correlates to his real-life circumstances.

What clues were given through-out the story to Peter's identity?

How did you feel about the ending? Did it satisfy you?

If you could write the conversation between Peter and Exa after the final scene, what would it say?

If you could change one scene in the book which one would it be? How would you change it and why?

What are any unanswered questions that you have?

How did you feel about the flashback scenarios? How did you feel about the multiple point of views? Why do you think the J.P. Sterling chose to structure the book that way?

I consider this novel to have a message of hope. What do you take away?

Did you find the plot predictable? If so, what scenes did you see coming and what were the clues? What scenes took you by surprise?

What is some of the symbolism J.P Sterling uses through-out the book? Does it contribute to the overall theme? Consider the title, did you find the symbolism to be fit or was it forced?

Has the novel changed or effected any of your previous opinions about anything?

If you were to talk with the author, what would you want to know? Guess what? I would love for you to invite me to your book club! Virtual arrangement can be made for me to visit with you by speaker phone or skype. Please don't hesitate to contact me @ jpsterling@jp-sterlingauthor.com or at my website www.jpsterling.com for a FREE ask-the-author book club virtual visit.

CPSIA information can be obtained
at www.ICGtesting.com
Printed in the USA
LVOW11s1516130617
537962LV00004B/703/P